THE TERROR OF THE SIMULACRA

OF THE

SIMULACRA

VOLUME ONE:
VITUPEROUS
CLEAVAGE

THE TERROR OF THE SIMULACRA

VOLUME ONE:
VITUPEROUS CLEAVAGE

ROSS CHANNING REED

OzarkMountainWritersGuild

Cover art and cover design by Nina Irwin

This is a work of fiction. All names, characters, incidents, and places are either created by the author or are used fictitiously, and any resemblance to anything in the real world, be it a living or dead person, a corporation or business establishment, an event, or a location is entirely coincidental.

Library of Congress Control Number: 2013952411

ISBN – 13: 978-1-940514-06-2

ISBN – 10: 1-940514-06-1

Ozark Mountain Writers Guild

Salem, Missouri 65560

ozarkmountainwritersguild@gmail.com

Also by Ross Channing Reed

Love and Death:
An Existential Theory of Addiction

A Philosopher Reports to Planet Earth:
Volume One

The Terror of the Simulacra:
Volume One: Vituperous Cleavage
Volume Two: Bulbous Chunks
Volume Three: Evisceration

Dedicated to Dr. John Ellsworth Winter and Dr. Richard J. Westley, freedom fighters.

CONTENTS

FOREWORD

In these United States, through diligence, perseverance, and hard work, we like to believe we have the opportunity to create our lives as we choose, in harmony with the interests of others. And if you happen to have the good fortune of a wealthy family, a first-tier college education (even if it's only as a legacy), and connections with powerful corporate interests, then the great brass ring called the American Dream is yours for the taking.

For the rest of us, the American Dream is an American Nightmare, thick with American Despair. If we are lucky, we get to work at two or three part-time jobs, without health benefits, with co-workers we want to choke and Powerball lotteries we can never seem to win. We work ourselves into early graves just to make ends meet, build relationships that make us long for the comfort of an asylum, eat bad and cheap fast food, clog our arteries, have strokes, have heart attacks, eat more fast crap, obsess over Hollywood celebrities, and do anything to be like those skinny supermodels who "have it all."

This book, the first volume in the *Terror of the Simulacra* trilogy (*Vituperous Cleavage, Bulbous Chunks, Evisceration*), is not meant for the faint of heart. It makes no appeal to a mass audience. Its audience is serious, but not solemn. Ostensibly a curious story about high school cross country runners, its protagonists convey energetic ideas and steadfast ideals readers will affectionately recognize as part of their own lives and, if you are who I think you are, continue to affirm today. At bottom, this book is for thoughtful readers, readers engaged in the art of living – a book for free spirits.

I met Ross Reed in Chicago in the fall of 1986. We were fellow graduate students in Loyola's doctoral philosophy program. We share an uncommon passion for existentialism – regarded by some "professional" philosophers as having already worn itself out as a philosophical movement. Of course, Ross and I both know this is patently false. The only philosophy worth its salt is lived philosophy, philosophy with its boots on the ground, dealing head on with those questions that continue to animate the human imagination. If you don't understand this, even if you have a Ph. D. in philosophy, you might *think* you're a philosopher, but trust me – you aren't.

Philosopher Reed's perception of the issues he presents in this book punches "conventional wisdom" in its collective face. He is uniquely qualified to make his case: he has supplemented his formal philosophical training with fifteen years plus as a philosophical counselor. He knows both the laudable and the loathing of what it means to be human, from both a theoretical and more importantly an experiential point of view. Contrary to popular belief, wealth and fame are not what life is about. Life is about family, life is about friends, life is about love. Be as cynical as you want – no one is more cynical than I am – but these are fundamental truths that none who are honest with themselves can deny. Against the backdrop of these truths we learn about Tommie, Monica, and the people that matter to them. With unflinching eyes we see in these characters' lives their pain, their goodness, their suffering, their beauty. This is the stuff meaning is made of, a few of the qualities that make life worth living. Like us, these kids and their families live in difficult economic times, where the American Dream is at best indefinitely delayed, more often altogether denied. Their stories present a reality far different from the media's derisive condescending portrayal of the Occupy Wall Street movement, dismissing the protests of "the ninety-nine percent" as the well-intentioned naïveté of ordinary people who just don't seem to be able to understand the intricate complexities of world finance.

I have the good fortune of being both a formally trained philosopher as well as a financial analyst with over fifteen years of experience with a global financial institution. I wanted to write this forward because this book squarely lands in the overlap that is, for better or worse, my life. I cannot emphasize enough the importance of the story you are about to read. If you suspect a handful of *über*-venture capitalists believe they are "too big to fail" and are gladly playing us for a bunch of fools, trust that intuition – it's remarkably close to the truth.

The Terror of the Simulacra is an all-too-human narrative of young hearts and minds facing the evil wrought by pathological greed. If you've ever wondered what "we are the 99 percent" really means, read this book. Its truth shines a sorely needed light on an inhumanity we need to grab by the throat and choke to death – before it kills us.

Chris "Breakneck" Broniak, Ph. D.
Chicago, Illinois

1

DON'T LET THE GONENESS TEAR YOU APART

You've got to be kidding me, I mean, there's no way that I should have to tell this story because there's no way this shit should ever have happened, I don't know, it's like the whole time it's happening you can't even believe it's real but then you realize it's your life and you can't go back and make it all disappear, that's just a pipe dream and it's all real and I know it's real 'cause I lived through it and I'm still standing, not quite as straight as before, but I've still got what's left of a voice and it's about time I use it and if I don't use it now I might as well give it up 'cause I mean what's the point in living if you don't stand for something and you don't say anything when it gets rough out there and all this weird-ass crap starts happening and you feel like pretty much your whole freakin' world is collapsing and you and everything you've ever known is going down down down? I mean, I used to be a regular guy on the cross-country team at Pine Manor, a little slower than most, but then the vortex started taking me down. Well, actually, like I said I was going down and everybody around me was going down, and there wasn't a damn thing we could do about it. We tried, oh yeah, don't get me wrong, we tried, but back then we still believed in the system. But that's all over now. And when it's over baby, it's over. Don't start whining over what you never had. It wasn't that great in the first place, so give up trying to get it back and face whatever you've got left that's real. Now, I'm out of the training wheels, but I don't know where the hell to go. I guess you could say I'm still in shock, but that's the nature of living in the 21st century. Get used to it. Shock is the new homeostasis. Quit your crying and start realizing you're on your own. Well, that's the story they'd like to tell, where it's an indelibly zero sum game. Some kind of horrific Hobbesian state of nature thing. Stop your ears to the damn propaganda machine and start looking at what's really going on. Who knows what the hell *is* really going on? And better yet, why? I hope I'm not the only one left. Okay, yeah, I'm not the only one. My brother Sammie is still here—basically—and Ferris. Either way, I'm feeling the blackness, so it's about time to get on with it. And besides, there are a lot of ways to crush a guy and some of 'em don't necessarily show up on the outside. Actually, I'd have to say most of 'em don't show up on the outside. At least not right away. Yeah maybe I'm telling this damn story because it's my story and the story of those I care about and somebody had to get it out there and who else was gonna do it? Before we decimate ourselves with progress and blow the planet right out of its somnambulistic orbit, that is. Maybe it's too late. I have no idea. All I know is some kind of freakin' fustercluck blew the hell out of what I thought life was all about, and I'm left here wondering: what's the point? It's a damn lonely planet when you don't know whom you can trust, or if you *did* know whom you could trust, but they're mostly gone. Yeah, that's what this story is about: goneness. There's so much goneness that I don't know if I can take it anymore. The goneness is the background for every breath you take. The goneness is a vacuum that slices through your heart, silently eviscerating your humanity. And yet, even with the ubiquitous goneness, we are somehow expected to get up the next morning, get dressed, eat breakfast, brush our teeth and go on with business as usual, just like the little automatons we were brought up to be. Right now, I feel like crying, but then my throat'll get all closed up like it usually does and I'll never get around to telling you the story. Thanks for listening. And if you're not listening, thanks for whatever the hell you're doing. Don't let the goneness tear you apart.

2

THE SECOND LONGEST PERIOD IN THE HISTORY OF THE WORLD

"C U @ the gym, loser."

Tommie slyly looked at the text while sitting in Lebowski's biology class, fourth period, the second longest period in the history of the world. Well, not literally, but anything before lunch seemed longer than a date with Valerie Brakefield. It was only 51 minutes, like every other waste of time period, but his mind was somewhere else. Not like that's particularly new or unusual, but really distracted, since there was a cross-country meet today against Lancaster Mennonite. It's not like the Mennonites were full of might—no, they were anything but mighty— but every race was a monstrous slog of pain and humiliation, especially if you sucked like Tommie. And the more you sucked, the longer the pain. As for the humiliation, that could last forever. His coach, Buffalo Bill (well, that's what they called him), used to joke with him: "Should I time you with a watch or with a calendar, Tommie?" Without a doubt, there were guys who sucked *more* than Tommie, but when you're out there sucking, the pain and suck factor are all your own. Let's face it, even with over-the-top pain management skills, some people just aren't good at sports—even sports that are mainly about pain management skills—since absence of talent always rears its heinous and harrowingly humiliating head. Blue-eyed Tommie is tall and lanky, with long, tangled, greasy blonde hair. With his practiced slouch, it is hard to tell if he is awake or asleep—especially on meet days, since he's trying to conserve energy. Why the heck was he on the damn team anyway? Some form of sadistic penance? Would they take anybody, literally anybody who was breathing? Yes, it was true that they would take anybody who was breathing, so that was a plus in Tommie's case. Why was he on the team? Let's see—for two reasons, both of them marginal. First there was this weird and otherworldly expectation and false belief on his part that you actually got out of it what you put into it, something he believed was untrue of most other "sports". What he really meant by this was that the sport didn't take any talent. If it were all effort and required absolutely no talent whatsoever, Tommie would be world class, given his ability to suffer. But he still sucked. And what inevitably made it worse was that he knew it. And he was *still* on the team. Some days, if it weren't for the girls team, almost everybody would be waiting on the bus before Tommie showed up at the finish line. The girls team. A blessing and a curse. It was a blessing, since the bus wouldn't actually leave without Tommie if there were still some girls out there. A curse if he ever got beaten by a...girl. That would be certain grounds for joining the chess team and saying goodbye to anything that involved sweat and competition. Hell, this "sport" seemed more like dog fighting—all contestants suffered, and almost nobody seemed to get out alive. At least, that's what it felt like, and when you're in high school, it's all about the feeling.

Oh, and that second reason. That second reason was his best friend, Ferris. They were both in the eleventh grade at Pine Manor. Ferris was about six inches shorter than Tommie, stocky and muscular, with brown hair that matched his eyes cropped close to his scalp. They ran together all year, and if for only an instant, as they slogged their eight minute miles over the Pennsylvania hills, they felt like they could conquer the world. At times, they got on each other's nerves, but not without an express purpose: to provide motivation to train harder and ultimately run faster at the season meets. Maybe even win a race or two, although that was, in a word, unlikely. Maybe against those mighty Mennonites? Nothing like creative visualization. And boy was it creative—although not ultimately effective. They say everybody's good at something.

Tommie always got so nervous that he could barely choke down any food the day of a meet. But if he didn't his blood sugar got so ridiculously low by 4:00 p.m. that he was combative, and when he tried to run he looked like a wounded water buffalo on oxycodone. Come to think of it, he pretty much looked like that even if he did eat lunch, which he basically didn't. This situation was a microcosm of life, or, you could say, an awesome life lesson: you're screwed either way. But giving up didn't seem any better, so Tommie packed his Asics racing flats and cross-country uniform at 7:15 a.m., just before he walked out the door with his older brother Sammie to head over to the high school, only a few blocks away. After fourth period biology, Tommie would see Ferris again at 2:30, since the "athletes" got out of last period fifteen minutes early—due to their privileged status as wanna be Greek gods, of course—but mostly since they had to be on the traveling team bus, which left before all the other buses. To most students at Pine Manor, athletes at least, cross-country runners didn't even count as athletes, but that's a different story. Cross-country runners were essentially invisible, except for their brief glory of getting to leave class fifteen minutes early on away meet days. Their self-designated godlike status was a well-hidden delusion, and getting to leave early certainly fed the flames—but it's not like the runners needed much evidence, since the delusion was based on faith alone. So they'd get out early, nursing their illusions of grandeur, and soon be headed to a world of pain and suffering. Buffalo Bill would have the chic yellow bus cranked up so that they could motor on over to the land of the Mennonites, all the way on the other side of Lancaster.

Tommie elbowed Ferris as soon as he saw the text. Then he wrote "IL KICK UR BUT BIGEST LOZR." For some reason, he was never able to successfully get the caps lock off, at least not while he was in class. He was technologically challenged. When Ferris saw the text, in his overtly covert way, under the double desk they shared, he tried to muffle the unmuffleable laugh. He started laughing and then almost crying, as Martial Law Lebowski turned around from writing his nonsense on the board. KINGDOM PHYLUM CLASS ORDER FAMILY GENUS SPECIES.

"Wow, I'm drinking up the knowledge," whispered Whiteson, from the double desk straight across, one row over toward the window. Tommie and Ferris started laughing and choking and choking and laughing and then suffocating and writhing around trying not to laugh or to choke or to suffocate. Lebowski, of course, turned red with anger. "You boys won't be laughing when you get down to the principal's office. March!" Well, the "march" order seemed even funnier than drinking up the knowledge, or even the lozer with the kicked but, so Tommie and Ferris were somehow paralyzed with laughter, as if their electrolytes were thoroughly depleted.

Forty-five seconds of silence, broken only with contorted efforts to muffle the laughter. By this time the third of the class who were (they thought) covertly texting, had stopped texting and all were sadistically transfixed on Ferris and Tommie.

"I'm sorry, Mr. Lebowski, but our electrolytes are so low that we can't even make it out of our seats" offered Tommie, completely ignoring the fact that Ferris's levity was so ebullient that he was beginning to feel unsteady in his seat.

"Wow, I'm drinking up the knowledge," whispered Whiteson, again. Ferris found Whiteson's sardonic remark so funny that he actually fell out of his chair, and onto the square foot tile floor, the kind with the oh-so-institutional look. School, prison, psych ward, the first being ample preparation for the rest.

"Holy crap, you bastard" said Ferris, in a voice supremely audible by all. Was it Tommie or Whiteson? Irrelevant, since he was screwed. Silence. Actually, somebody must've had their clandestine ear buds in, because you could hear "Teenage Dream" playing in the back half of the room.

Luckily, Lebowski was half deaf, or just dumb, or just smart. Well, how smart could he be if he was voluntarily spending the rest of his life in…school?

A digression, surely, but that seemed to be the essence of their lives.

"You guys suck. Dumb asses. Get a life," Lentzeimer chimed in, filled with a palpable lack of empathy and a not-so-secret glee.

Lebowski was frozen in space, staring straight at Tommie and Ferris since he'd uttered the word "march". He was waiting for some kind of a response from the instigators. No doubt a preamble for after-school suspension, thought both Tommie and Ferris—and there goes the meet. The laughter was dying down into a seeping fear. They both knew what this might mean. Buffalo Bill wasn't going to be happy at all. Not at all. Or maybe he was. When you sucked as much as Tommie and Ferris, being left behind could be a...good thing. And they both knew it. Oh well, there's always next year. Meanwhile, Lebowski was still staring. It was the biology class to remember. Or not remember. Tommie was thinking to himself that *he* might be out of the hot seat, so to speak, since *Ferris* was literally out of his seat. Maybe Lebowski would nail Ferris and leave him out of it. But then Kohrner, double desk aft, farted. It wasn't your average fart either. It was long and sticky, a good four seconds, and about five girls yelled out "gross" before the thing had a chance to stop reverberating off of the oh-so-institutional walls.

Katy Perry was still playing softly in the background. Tommie started laughing so hard he would have been asphyxiated if the atmospheric oxygen dropped even one percentage point lower than its customary twenty-one percent. But then, the divine eyes rested upon Tommie and Ferris. They were delivered from the hand of the fowler.

There was yelling in the hall. Followed by more yelling. A brief pause, and then the yelling got louder. This distracted Lebowski. Five foot, six inch 130 pound Lebowski with the pencil thin moustache was going to go out into the hall to see about the ruckus. Yeah, he'll see about the ruckus. He opened the door, stepped out, and started his authoritative thought police routine that they all knew so well. SLAM! The beakers and glass equipment in the windowed wall cases against the hallway wall shook like crazy. SLAM! More rocking beakers and such. More yelling, but it wasn't Lebowski. Before they knew it, Head Principal Trout stuck his head in doorway, out of breath, instructing them to remain calm.

"Wow, I'm drinking up the knowledge," whispered Whiteson for the third time, in a smooth deadpan.

"Is there anything you don't drink? Meier asked, with oozing mockery.

"Shut up, you wuss ass. Why don't you go collect a few stamps?"

Whiteson didn't whisper this time. It was true, Meier was the school king of stamp collecting. A small kingdom, but still. Oh, and the French horn too. Probably an even smaller kingdom.

After the commotion dies down, Principle Trout finally walks in. He informs the class that school officials have called 911 and that biology class is still in session, even though their instructor will not be returning. Later, they learned that Wade Stephenson was being expelled and was engaging in a shouting match with the principal as he headed down the hallowed main hall for his final time. Then Lebowski got in his face and ended up with the short end of the stick. Really short. So short that an ambulance had to cart him away with injuries to his face and torso. He missed three days of school, and when he came back, he didn't want to talk about it.

They had a sub for two weeks. Miss Bonaventure. But that's another story. Let's just say that Tommie and Ferris *didn't* get after school suspension, and *did* get to run in the meet, if you could call it running. It certainly wasn't making the world a better place. Ferris was faster than Tommie for about the first ninety seconds of the five kilometer race, what with his superior percentage of white fast twitch muscle fibers, meaning that Tommie was faster than Ferris for about the last 1140 seconds of the race, the 1140 that actually counted. Tommie has about zero percent fast twitch muscle fibers, meaning he went out slow and had no kick. Spectacular. Ferris, on the contrary, went out like a shot—for 117 meters, then cramped up and ran with his shoulders up to his ears for 4,789 meters—and then sprinted like the Olympic 200 meter final for the last ninety-four meters.

As for the meet with Lancaster Mennonite, they were victorious in two senses: both finished the race, *and* no girls beat them, so they didn't have to move to a new state. On the other hand, Klinefelter was the only male "runner" to finish after them, and he was slow even for him. Maybe he got lost, which is not so bad if it leads to an inadvertent shortcut, which didn't seem to be the case for Klinefelter.

Sometimes they wondered if he'd know a shortcut if he saw one. Before every meet, Buffalo Bill would speak in a serious monotone, as he looked through his fat plastic glasses with the strap on the back: "Run the shortest legal distance without stopping." That "without stopping" part sure was a high bar, and besides, if you were walking, you weren't stopping. It just made for a damn long 5K, and you'd want to finish with a bag over your head.

3

TO AVRIL OR NOT TO AVRIL

I'm in bed with Avril Cheyenne. I can hardly believe it. I slap myself just to make sure it's real. We're at a log cabin. Outside, it's snowing. I see distant mountains. I see a fireplace with a roaring fire.

I ask Avril: "Are you Avril Cheyenne?"

"Who did you expect? Lady Gaga?"

"No, I mean, are you really Avril Cheyenne? If you're not, you could have fooled me." My head is spinning and I'm starting to feel really stupid—not that unusual—but I realize I'm stupid and naked at the same time, in bed with an Avril Cheyenne look alike. That was unusual, even for me. Holy crap. I'm thinking it's like I'm dreaming or something. Then Avril (we'll call her that for the sake of brevity) looks at me with a pissed off look, pulls off the covers and jumps out of bed, cat walking toward the bathroom, absolutely naked. I'm feeling some serious warmth in the groinial area. Dios mio, get back in the bed Avril. Please. Help me. I'm feeling the major woody. I'm getting that familiar feeling of really screwing up a great opportunity, for example, the great opportunity to sleep with Avril Cheyenne. What is my freakin' problem? Do I really care if it's not Avril if it looks like Avril? I mean if it looks like Avril and it talks like Avril, do I really need DNA testing before we jump in the sack? I can tell you this much: I know *my* answer. And in this case, we were already in the sack. Maybe we *already* did it? That would be just like me, not remembering the main act. But we probably didn't do it, since I would have absolutely no idea of what to do. Maybe Avril took advantage of me? One can only hope.

Avril catwalks out of the bathroom, toward me, and gets right back into bed. I now know that there is a God.

She rolls over toward me, with her face only inches from mine. "Do you want to do it again…like last time?" she whispers, licking her lips and getting way too close. Her black hair falls over the left side of her face. You'd need a million bucks and a dozer to get me out of this bed, and without the dozer, there'd be no way.

"Like like like last time?" I ask. Man am I a dork. She rolls over and faces the wall. It's still snowing outside. And damn if it isn't starting to snow inside. Right now, I'll bet 50% of my blood is in my private part. An interminable silence.

"Avril, I want to do it—like last time," I say like a star quarterback, affecting the deepest possible believable voice.

"Oh *really*?" she says, in a mocking tone, still facing the wall. She rolls back over and faces me, with her head on her pillow. She's giving me a pointed look. "Do you want to do it with *Avril*, or do you want to do it with *me*? I can't give you what you want if you want to do it with Avril, and I'm not Avril," she crows.

"That's true," I say, speaking very slowly, trying to be conciliatory. "But I want to do it with *you.*"

She lifts her head off the pillow and looks me in the eyes. I feel her legs moving under the covers, touching mine. "Have you got protection?"

As if we didn't wake up in bed stark naked.

"Uh, protection?" I'm now the official king of dork. I don't know who I'm with, I don't know where I am, I don't even know if I've brought a toothbrush, and now she wants to know if I've got protection?

"No delection if there's no protection," she says, head back on the pillow, staring at the ceiling.

There used to be a God. Anyway— delection? Is that a word? My man parts are starting to ache like they've never ached before. Either way, I doubt that I'll ever recover.

"Have you been tested?" she asks, sounding an awful lot like a freakin' public service announcement. God, this hurts—in so many ways.

"Tested? That's all I've been—tested, tested, tested, tested right out the wazoo. It feels like I've got something up my rectum all day and all night, just to keep everybody happy. Life is like one big proctologist's examining room, with everybody examining the shit out of you, when they're all full of shit themselves."

Avril liked that a lot more than anything I've said so far. Wow, I didn't know I could seduce women with talk of colonoscopies. Who knew? I thought that *she* was supposed to blind me with science. Lebowski comes into my head. Get out, you bastard, get out, I'm busy with things that are a lot more important than you.

I notice a night stand on my side of the bed. Is this a one night stand or just one night stand? I roll over and open the single slim drawer, and I notice a ten-pack of heavy duty ultra condoms, below which is a piece of paper with officious looking writing on it. I unfold it, and see test results from a clinic. My name is at the top of the page. HIV – neg. *Dios mio—there is a God.* I look at the condoms, the paper, and am dumbfounded. Now, *all* of my blood has rushed from my head to the netherpart. Then I start to smile, slowly, like a coyote. I almost cry with joy.

I take the ten-pack and the clinic result, and slowly lean over toward Avril. She takes them in her hands and looks at them as if they were moon rocks. Her head begins to pivot in my direction. Then she starts to smile, slowly, like a coyote.

"What was your name again? she asks. She is staring straight at me with her penetrating aquamarine eyes. Then she breaks into "Don't Wanna Be Your Dipshiitake."

There is a God, and he has created Avril Cheyenne. And she is here in bed with me. I will be saved.

I wake up. I'm late for school. I'm not naked. It's not snowing outside. There is no fire in the nonexistent fireplace. And Avril is not in bed with me.

4

STURM UND DRANG

I got my fat ass out of bed at the crack of fucking dawn and got ready for the cattle-call parade of losers that passes for the goddamn public high school. When I got there and walked the hell in, I got the same fucked up feeling I always get, like there's some kind of freakin' sensory overload goin' on just lookin' at the weird shit goin' down in the hall. I mean, first of all, you've got like 10,000 *too many fuckers* in this joint to start with and if it'd be a prison they'd at least be in *cells*, but here, no—no, in here they get to wander free like the circus freaks they are. So, the hall's fuckin' packed with people and I'm about ready to pass out just trying to push my way through all the bastards. I mean, what the hell, losers doing the fucking lip lock like right in the middle of the freakin' hall like they couldn't do it outside or in some car or some ditch or who the hell cares where—just anyplace but here, how about that? So, it's hell just trying to get to your goddam locker. Not like I really want to, but you know how it is. I'd like to get a shirt that says in big bold letters NOBOBY FUCKS WITH MONICA LeBLANC. But it'd never pass the dress code.

So when I get there and finally push my way down the hall, opening the ass wipe locker is another thing entirely, it's like you gotta clear out the riff raff just to get the stupid skinny shitass metal door open. Maybe I won't even get that far.

I'm barely in the front door as it is. So, I'm walkin' in the front door and who do I see? Mindy goddamn junior prom queen Edgerton-Rumpf. God, I hate those fucking hyphenated names. Like I'm gonna waste six shitty syllables just saying her name. Okay, mine's five, but you get the point. Shit. Give me a break.

Okay, but Me-lin-da makes it seven. So Me-lin-da Edgerton-Rumpf is standing just inside the entrance to the proto-penitentiary, leaning against a fuckin' faux-marble column doing the liplock with football star asshole Joe Buckius. She's trying not to cry over spilled milk and he's trying to keep it in his pants. She's probably workin' on makin' herself feel a whole lot better after dumping the baby last year. Yeah, that's the way to start out *right* in life. Have sex with some loser, get pregnant, and then bump off *your own* kid. And then spend the rest of your pathetic life trying to make yourself feel okay about it, telling yourself you did the right thing for your "future". Right. You *bumped off* your own kid. That was probably your *first real action* as a grownup, and what did you do? Knocked off your own kid. Wow. Yeah, go get yourself a whole goddamn box of gold stars for that one. Wouldn't want to fuck up *your* future. What's in *your* future? Oh. Right. More *education*. You want to finish your *education*. This *is* your *education*, bitch! Listen up. *Your education* is the fact that you're 16 and pregnant and the father is even more immature than you are so you're up shit creek without a goddamn paddle. So, I guess it's time to bump somebody off so you can get yourself out of a jam. Yeah, that's it. Or did you think that life on this planet was so goddamn shitty that you didn't want to bring the poor bastard into it? Is that it? Well, if so, what the hell are *you* doing here? You didn't bump *yourself* off, now did you? Oh, I forgot. You're here for more education. Yeah. That's it. And while I'm at it—thanks to all the grownups for all that swell guidance. Shit. Are we on our own here? Fuck, my eyes still can't adjust to the dim light in this hellhole and it looks like a freak show Halloween extravaganza. Edgerton-Rumpf and Joe Buckius. Bunch of dipshits. But that's just for starters. God. Get me the fuck out of here.

And then there's the plain old bullshit phoney chicks all over the place just trying to live up to their charade. Hey, it's not like you have to look hard to explain suburbia. It's right here in front of you, waiting to happen, with a stockade fence around your bigass landscaped yard, a goddamn electric gate out front with a security code, guard, and a piece of shit alarm system on every ticky-tacky shithouse in slimytown. Oh, and the underwater mortgage waiting to happen.

I'm feeling fat as hell today. No sense in hiding it. I feel like a fuckin' beached walrus globally warmed into a crisp and about ready to burst with gastric juices and bile. Yee-haw. I know I'm gonna be learnin' so much today that I stayed up all night just thinking about it. Okay, that was bullshit. Another fucking year, here we are again, and what's changed? Oh, I forgot, it's getting worse by the minute. Wait a minute. Alert the press. It's fucking walrus fatass Monica Leblanc, rolling in for another year of learning the shit out of everything there is to learn. Yee-haw.

I'm trying to walk the fuck past the heavy druggie section, but it's hard as hell. I don't know what the fuck they're doing, showing off some new goth playtoy or what, but I wish they'd just get the fuck out of my way. Poor bastards won't have much brain activity left by the time they're outta here, graduation or no. Prison? Death? Who the hell knows? Couldn't be worse than it was for Edgerton-Rumpf-Buckius. So the druggies are the cool as hell I-want-to-fuckin'-blow-my-brains-before-I-blow-puberty crowd and I just don't get it. Besides standing in my way when I'm trying to get to my locker, they're blowing just about the only ticket they've got to get the hell outta this place. I mean, it's not exactly subversive to blow *your own* brain. It's just fuckin' stupid. We're the subversive in that?

And if you're that dumb *before* you start to take drugs…I can only imagine.

So, I pushed my way through the smell of pot and cigarettes and cheap underarm deodorant and shitty cologne and rancid body odor and finally made it to my locker. It's only like 7:35 in the morning and I'm ready for a nap. I don't care how long it is. A lifetime would be fine. Just get me the fuck out of here. Yeah, okay, I mean I'm right here and there's like ten people crowded up against the lockers doing who knows what with who knows who and I'm just trying to get to my fucking locker so I don't have to carry all this shit around all day. Can't I at least put my fatass lunch in my locker? I mean, c'mon. I just can't *believe* this is my life. I keep pushing until I get to my locker, open the lock and get my shit out of my backpack and stuff it in my locker. I don't look at anybody but I do smell a lot of bad breath and stupidity.

Then I push my way to the bathroom so I don't piss myself during Sociology or English Lit. The seat is cold as hell, but taking a piss is about the most fun I've had all day. Linda Fowler was in there too, in the handicapped stall. She's in this wheelchair now after the wreck last spring. Riding in the back seat after some big shot party and some drunken asshole crashed the car down near Slackwater and killed two kids.

Maybe Fowler was lucky. She can't walk anymore, but she can move her arms. She says "Hi" to me now, ever since the accident. Sometimes she even says "Hi Monica." I say "Hi" back. Sometimes I even say "Hi Linda". In the scheme of things, we're both basically invisible. Well, today we ended up both looking into the mirror at the same time. I noticed she was crying but I didn't say anything. We both kept staring straight ahead into the mirror.

"Why do people have to be so…mean? Why?" she asked with a kind of wimper. We both continued to stare straight ahead, but our eyes met in the mirror.

"I don't know, Linda. I don't know," I said.

I held the door open for her as she rolled on out.

5

LIKE THERE'S NO TOMORROW

Harlan is playing Barnacle Soufflé on his dad's ancient sound system when Tommie shows up. *Shooby dooby dooby where the hell would you be?....I been lookin' all over for the four leaf clover....Ain't seen nothin' but a busted up studmuffin....Shooby dooby dooby where where where the hell would you be?....I be lookin' I be livin' but there ain't noboby givin'....It's been way too long with this pocket jive song....gotta find a reason to keep going on....* It was 9:30 a.m. on Saturday, almost the middle of the night for Harlan. He's trying to wake up. His dirty blonde hair looks like a rooster back. He is barely conscious, even with the speakers within inches of his head. Clearly additional evidence for the anecdotal truth that some teenagers can't learn until after lunch, if ever. He's so skinny that his knee joints bulge out at the bottom of his thighs. He turns down the music when he sees Tommie.

"Hey Harlan dude, what's up? What's up, man?" Harlan lies motionless in his protracted pusillanimity. Tommie kicks a metal leg of the bed and keeps talking. "Why you always play that classic rock shit? Barnacle Soufflé? It's like Neanderthal rock. Literally stone age. Those dudes are like a hundred years old or something. Have you seen a picture of Foobar Freshass lately? He looks like a cross dressing geriatric. Or maybe just French dressing. He's older than your dad.

Foobar, the old bastard," Tommie laughs, mostly to himself, thinking about all the old times listening to Barnacle Soufflé. Tommie looks down at Harlan, who appears to be somewhere between unconsciousness and death, on the folding bed that is actually a cot with a lumpy and at the same time thin mattress. The Precambrian rock continued to reverberate. Apparently, Harlan's parental units were down with noise. They didn't put many restrictions on Harlan, even if everyone suffered.

"Uuff." Harlan eyes look like they're pasted shut. He doesn't speak for at least fifteen seconds and then slowly half whispers, half mumbles "Come on, man, it's like I learned to like it from my dad. He has a lot of old CDs and crap, and even old records. The cover art is awesome on those records. And c'mon, you know you like it, be-atch."

"If we were busted up studmuffins we'd still be a whole lot faster than we are now, wouldn'tya say? Even a busted up studmuffin is still a studmuffin, which we definitely are not," says Tommie, stepping over piles of clothes and books strewn all over the small floor.

"Face it, assmunch, you just suck. You'd need to make a pact with the devil just to pass me, and I suck," opines Harlan, sitting upright and rubbing his eyes.

"Maybe he'd give us all magic powers, so we could blow right by Hempfield, those pussies."

"You mean powers like God isn't giving us now?" quips Harlan. "Besides, they may be pussies, but what does that make us? All we see in a race is their skinny asses. Especially if we're talking about you."

"Good point, Debbie Downer. Thanks and you suck."

"Okay, yeah, but even then it's mainly *me* looking at their skinny asses, since you're way too far behind to see. You'd need a freakin' telescope," said Harlan, yawning.

"Where's Ferris?"

"I called him, man, last night. He'll be here. I just hope he has a few bills," says Harlan.

It's true. Ferris is dependable. He'll be there. And he may have a few bills.

"Shooby dooby dooby where where where the hell would you be?....I be lookin' I be livin' but there ain't noboby givin'....You got to get here....before I have another...." Foobar Freshass chimes in.

Harlan lives in a rental apartment in a four flat, rare enough to find in this town. The yard, if you could call it that, is unkempt, peppered with wind-strewn pockets of trash. The building looks as close to a tenement as you are going to find in these parts. No pride of ownership here. The occasional graffiti adorns its brick façade. It's usually rented by college students, but his whole family lives here. His dad is an English Professor at the University, his mother is an artist, and his sister is a pain in the ass. The whole place is barely 500 square feet, with Harlan's room being a spacious seventy-two of these. Harlan's room is actually more like a walk-in closet, except you'd be walking into it from the hallway. His room is across the hall from his sister's, a colossal thirty-six inches away.

Shooby dooby dooby where the hell would you be?....I been lookin' all over for the four leaf clover....Ain't seen nothin' but a busted up studmuffin....Shooby dooby dooby where where where....

His dad has a one year contract at the university, which is a euphemism for a nine-month contract, so there's no point in trying to buy a house, even though it's a buyer's market, what with prices dropping a good twenty percent since '06. They've moved eight times since Harlan was born in 1996. Six one-year contracts that weren't renewed, two one-year contracts that were renewed one time each, and one one-year contract that was renewed twice.

Colleges and universities have gradually realized that they can eliminate tenure track positions and replace them with permanent temporary professors (in the language of Newspeak), now *well over* seventy-five percent of all faculty in higher education. As long as the public (especially the parents who pick up the tab) doesn't catch wind of it, the schools can pretend that their "product" is just as good as it was before—if the schools were ever, at any point, in the business of education. There is a major cost savings for the institutions, and they don't have to worry about any push back from the professors, since academic freedom will only exist in memory (if at all), as will the necessary grounds for a free society. Hence, the institutions of higher education in a free society finally create the conditions through which they destroy the very possibility of free society. They contradict their express mission in order to ensure their survival, if survival of the university is what we are witnessing now. Maybe the university in America died long ago, and this is only the terror of the simulacra. Anyway, the sharecropper professors have generally learned to shut up and pretend to teach the ill-equipped students as if they were real students, and if these permanent temporaries uncharacteristically *don't* remain silent about the actual issues, their contracts (such as they are) will, mysteriously, not be renewed. Dr. Harlan was only one among thousands nationwide who suffered from such mysterious nonrenewal. And so the academic migrants go from one state to the next, hoping to buck the ever-longer odds, their families in tow, all suffering from something that they will never understand. Awash in the inhumane, they toil daily to teach the humanities to increasingly desperate and marginally literate post-9/11 college students in a world gone crazy with violence and dread. They try desperately to block consciousness of the irony, but how long can anyone keep up the charade before overwhelmed with suffering and emptiness?

People around here say Dr. Harlan is lucky to have the one-year, since there is an army of adjuncts with semester-by-semester, course-by-course contracts, unilaterally rescindable up until the first day of classes. The whole Harlan family is kind of skittish, since they have to think about moving whenever they make *any* other decision. Just being over there at the apartment, Tommie senses impermanence and instability. There are also the obvious unpacked boxes in corners. Maybe they stay that way. Why unpack if you're moving in nine months or twenty-one months, or whatever? Besides, you probably won't need that shit anyway if you're headed for a homeless shelter.

When Harlan showed up on the scene last August for summer cross-country practice, everybody thought he was maybe a little stupid.

Then everybody learned his dad was an English Professor, which, of course, didn't settle the issue. He's been here sixteen months now. His dad is getting ready to send out another round of dossiers, writing samples, and letters of recommendation and hope that he can grovel his way through another Modern Language Association convention cattle call during the holidays. Harlan can't remember three of the eight places he's lived.

"Get your running crap on, dude, unless you're gonna run in your boxers" cajoles Tommie.

Harlan stumbles back into the room after taking a much needed piss. He always seems to be shaky in the mornings (the evenings aren't so great either) so there's always piss around the rim when he's shakin' it off, but sometimes it's a lot more than just the rim. In the mornings, when the east sun hits the bowl just right, you can see the effulgence of copious yellowish-amber liquid grace vast portions of the porcelain—and not just the porcelain.

Tommie is outfitted and ready to go, so they can get back and get on over to the House of Pizza, if funds allow it.

....*gotta find reason to keep going on*....

"I can't find my other running shoe. Crap," says Harlan, crawling under his desk. There's a loud cracking sound as he hits his head on the underside of the cheap, small but heavy fiberboard desk. "Shit. Shit. Ooww." He pops back up rubbing his head with one hand, the running shoe in the other. "What's the temperature?"

"It's about 57 or 58 degrees, just perfect, bonehead," says Tommie, shaking his head and looking at Harlan with amusement. "Or it *was* perfect, if we ever get out of here, dude."

"You mean Millersville? I thought you liked it here. Anyway, we've got to wait for Ferris, dude, so chill out."

"No dude, I mean if we ever get out on the road. And how would I know if I like Millersville? I mean, I've got like nothing to compare it to, right? You're the one that's lived in sixty-seven places or whatever."

"I get it. Watch it with the ambiguity. Anyway, it's nine places. I've lived nine places, counting here." Harlan fumbles to get both shoes on his feet. Not only can he not multi-task, he can barely mono-task.

"OK, nine. Eight more than I have. Anyway, *your* dad is the English Professor, Shakespeare. I'm just a busted up studmuffin wanna be."

Harlan laughed. "No argument here, Foobar."

"Oh yeah, I'm the rock star Foobar.

"Oh yeah! Oh yeah! And you're just a skinny chicken breast wanna be."

Shooby dooby dooby where where where the hell would you be?....I be lookin' I be livin' but there ain't noboby givin'....It's been way too long with this pocket jive song....gotta find reason to keep going on...."

Tommie looks out the small window and then looks at Harlan as he finally ties up his running shoes. "Where do you want to go, anyway?"

"Ah, let's go down Stehman's Road," offers Harlan.

"Cool, but I'm not calling 911 if you can't make it, buttmunch. What if Ferris doesn't want to do it?"

"He should have gotten here earlier. We'll just mock him until he gets pissed off and his adrenaline kicks in and he'll make it. That's what friends are for. But take your phone anyway, just in case." To Tommie, Harlan's summary seemed irrefutable.

Tommie already has his phone in a plastic bag under his spandex shorts. He's got nylon shorts overtop, just to keep away the women, or in case the spandex gives way. His phone is turned off, but it's not like anybody is calling.

There is clomping on the steps. Ferris walks in, looking like a cross between a superhero and a clown.

....I be lookin' I be livin' but there ain't noboby givin'....

"Holy crap, dudes, that music is so...fossilized. And cool. Barnacle Soufflé? What the? Anybody ready for pizza?" Ferris says with a grin, his nylon shorts twisted so that the tag is sticking out almost at his right hip.

"Ferris! You loser! Figures you're ready to go straight for the food. You've got to run first. Not that you've ever done *that* before. Yeah, we're ready. Right after the easy ten miler." Harlan has his shoes on—triple tied—his running singlet is on—inside out— and his blood sugar is up to 41, without a doubt. Ferris has a plastic gallon jug of Sweet Tea. The easy ten miler could turn out to be neither. And the House of Pizza seems like another lifetime.

"Okay, Ferris, you can run with us...if you can keep up," Harlan says sarcastically, eyeing the tea. Ferris rips the top off and slugs a good quart of the stuff, belches, and then passes the offering to Tommie.

"I can always take a leak in a cornfield," says Ferris, emitting an even louder sharp edged burp.

"Or in your pants," mocks Harlan. He knows that if he doesn't shut up, he's not going to be able to drink any of their favorite swill. He's on the verge now, and he knows it. It's obvious that he is now awake, awake enough to agitate Ferris. But he could probably do that in his sleep.

Shooby dooby dooby where where where the hell would you be?....I been waitin' I been hating on this lonely ass gratin'....UUhh UUhh UUhh UUhh UUhh UUhh UUhh UUhh.... Yeah baby yeah baby....shooby dooby dooby give me some of that pooty....

"I'll probably just piss on you. Okay, maybe not, because you'll be so far behind that I won't be able to hold it that long." Touché. Ferris steps up to the plate. Then he passes the jug off to Harlan. They keep passing the jug around, Harlan finishes it off, crumples it up and puts the cap back on.

They shuffle down the narrow hall, passing Dr. Harlan in the living room study, who is staring at a pile of papers through his wire spectacles. The professor mumbles something about being careful, but doesn't look up. Harlan leads the exit through the back door, makes a jump shot and lobs the jug right past the recycling container.

"Better stick with cross-country. At least you can beat Klinefelter. So far." Ferris is killing it. He'll pay later, when he's got no cover, somewhere out on the undulating, tarry, sticky, crowned, narrow country roads. He's already feeling it.

They hit the street, and as they start running, everything seems alright, if only for a moment.

6

ATTACK CHIHUAHUA

"Slow it down! Slow it down! What's this race business?" Ferris yells. Two minutes into the run and Ferris is already irritated—and thirty meters behind Tommie and Harlan. Suddenly, Ferris is at a near sprint. He settles in just behind Tommie and Harlan, with rasping breath. "Can't you just start out slow? I can't stand going into oxygen debt in the first block. We don't need to train for anaerobic metabolism. Buffalo Bill training gives us plenty of that," puffs Ferris. He'll go out fast in a race, but in your everyday run, he slogs it from beginning to end. But suddenly, he passes them as they top the hill at West Cottage Avenue, leading by a meter or two. He's breathing hard but doesn't say anything. He looks straight ahead.

"Cut the exercise physiology crap. You're just a wuss. Your motto is start slow and taper off. At least, that's what you do every race. That's because you suck. Yeah, you suck big time," taunts Tommie, now from behind. He's a damn fine coach. As a motivational speaker, not so much.

They cross the four way together as they descend Prince Street. Something's always going on at the university, and as they slab the edge of campus, today appears to be no exception. They pretend not to see the women, but then it's too much.

"I'm sure glad I'm not gay," says Ferris

with a little less of a puff, clearly having regained his blood oxygen. Or not. All three heads are turned to the spectacle across the street.

"What, rock star?" asks Harlan, seeking clarification for the absurd, clearly the son of an English Professor. "Who says you're not gay?"

"Let's just say that even if I *were* gay, those women over by the dorm would still look *hot*."

"Oh, so you're *not* saying that you're *not* gay," says Harlan, the prince of deconstruction.

"Shut up. I'm not gay, dumbass. You know what I mean." Ferris has both Asics GT-2050s in his mouth, and he keeps speaking. *Ad hominem*.

"We know that you haven't gotten any action in, what would you say, Tommie? Sixteen years? Yeah. Sixteen years."

Tommie grunts affirmatively, still looking across the street, back over his shoulder. The spectacle has elided into the past.

Ferris's shoes are slapping the ground even more than usual. He's grimacing.

"Okay, Ferris, we're all losers. Do you feel better now? But you're the biggest loser." Harlan is really working Ferris over, and Tommie is really enjoying it. Two more blocks have gone by. They pass the House of Pizza as they turn west on Frederick Street.

"He's just kidding," Tommie says, looking over at Ferris to see if he is going to cry.

"I know, but I'm not gay," says Ferris, almost in a whine. No doubt he will recover by the time they get back to the House of Pizza—on the way back *into* town, but that's a long time from now. Ferris continues to slap forward, head down, a defeated expression on his face.

"Would it really matter if you were gay, dude? You'd still suck just as much at cross-country," says Tommie, suggesting both the hypothetical and not so hypothetical.

"Hey, I don't have anything *against* gayness. *You* can be gay all you want. Gay people are okay. I just don't want to be gay, okay? My life is hard enough as it is, without having to be gay too, you know? I like chicks," says Ferris, underscoring his refrain. He's got his second wind, all in seven minutes. He'll need at least three or four more, because there's a lot of hilly road to go.

"So, you're saying that if you *were* gay, which you're not, you wouldn't like it? asks Tommie, quizzically, looking over at Ferris, wondering when he's going to realize he'd be better off if he just shut up.

"Dude, I already said that. If *you* want to be gay, go right ahead. I don't care if your whole family wants to be gay. Go right ahead. *I* just don't want to be gay. And if I *were* gay, which I'm *not*, I wouldn't like it. I'd want to be straight," says Ferris with an edge of anger, exhibiting what might pass for fundamentalist certitude as he barks it out between breaths. His breathing has mutated into a high-pitched nasal whine.

"If you're not gay, how do you know that you wouldn't like it if you were gay? queries Harlan. "How can you know you wouldn't like it if you don't even know what it's like? Maybe gayness is what you're missing. Ever thought about that, dude?" Tommie and Ferris seem to miss a step together, and they look at Harlan, who is in between them, as if he's gay. Ferris is thinking about Harlan's line of questioning as they cruise through the lovely Brookwood apartments, on the southwest edge of town, but his brain is shutting down.

"*No*, I've never thought about that, sphincter brain. Why in hell would I think about *that*? I can't imagine *how* I would like to be gay. It sounds like it sucks. No, it sucks, dude, it sucks," Ferris says emphatically, looking confused and then resuming his downward glance as they pound the pavement.

"Ferris, dude, you're just saying that since you're not attracted to men, it seems like it sucks to be attracted to men," replies Harlan, uncovering a hidden tautology. He goes on: "Do you like asparagus, Ferris?"

"You know I hate asparagus. But what's your point? C'mon. Just shut up and run."

"I hate it too," says Tommie. "But I *love* pizza."

"Shut up, dumbasses, why don'tcha. Just shut up," says Ferris, almost pleading.

"Thanks for that, Tommie. But let's focus on Ferris. We still know he's not gay, right?" continues Harlan, ignoring Ferris' pleas for silence. "Okay, Ferris, so you hate asparagus. Now imagine that you *like* asparagus. How is it?"

"Harlan, you loser, *I don't like asparagus.* What's wrong with you, dude? How can I imagine that I like what I don't like? That's just stupid and dumb too."

"Stupid *and* dumb. Wow. That's bad. So, if we wanted to talk with someone who *liked* asparagus, *you* wouldn't be the guy. We'd have to find somebody who actually *liked* asparagus, right?" says Harlan, invigorated. Harlan had to expend very little energy to keep up the pace, being the better runner, so he had a great deal more in reserve to agitate his friends, and they knew it, hoping against hope that he would just shut up and run. But both also knew that there was no chance that Harlan was going to shut up, so they just tried to appease him as best as possible.

"I thought we were talking about being gay, and you're talking about asparagus," says Ferris, annoyed. It is now obvious that Ferris doesn't like men or asparagus. "Nobody's attracted to asparagus, dude. C'mon and get off it." This point, a *prima facie* victory, had yet to be determined, what with the polyperversity of humankind. Ferris was losing focus, but he literally couldn't get away, so Harlan kept up the hammering. Meanwhile, Ferris' shorts were riding up his buttcrack, but no one, apparently, noticed. Not like it was unusual.

The pace was quickening as a result of the discussion. And there was still a long way to go.

"I guess you like asparagus, Harlan you bastard?" Ferris almost yells, gasping for oxygen. The slapping seems to be getting louder and louder.

"Nope, I hate asparagus," Harlan deadpans.

Ferris rolls his eyes to the left, giving the now clearly insane Harlan a wide berth.

They turn left onto Duke Street, passing the site of the old Amos Funk's Farm Market. It's a long slog down through the valley, over the Conestoga River, and past Slackwater. Ferris may be gay by then. The few clouds are hanging high in the sky, making it look like anything's possible.

"Okay, Ferris, I'll shut up about the asparagus. It sucks anyway. You believe in God, right?" asks Harlan, never one to quit before it's too late.

"Dude, first it's gayness, then asparagus, now God? What the hell? Are you going to tell me that God is gay and likes asparagus?" says Ferris, incredulously looking over at Harlan. It won't be long until they hit the hill at Slackwater. It's a long tough climb out of the Conestoga River valley up to the ridge. It won't be easy to concentrate on God, gayness and asparagus.

"Harlan, you ought to be an interrogator for Homeland Security," says Tommie, who was always trying to make it easier for those who suffered, even if he had caused the suffering in the first place. The running, of course, was the easy part.

"I'd be too good. Probably have to start my own country."

"How 'bout your own planet? You can beam there right now, and then you won't have to run up to Long Lane," offers Ferris, slapping his feet with abandon. He's got the look runners get when they'd prefer to run alone. "Ur-ANUS is already taken," he says, affecting a feeble laugh.

"YOUR-anus is taken, that's for sure," says Tommie, no longer making it easy for those who suffered.

"Okay, dudes, okay. Enough artifice with the orifice. It ain't gonna kill you to talk about it, and you're not going to turn gay, and neither is God," says Harlan, ignoring the banter. "C'mon Ferris, you believe in God, right dude? Could you decide to stop believing in God?"

"What is *that* supposed to mean, dumbass? You know I believe in God," says Ferris, irritated by the usual triumvirate: low blood sugar, lack of oxygen to the brain, and a couple of assholes for running buddies. He looks like he's getting ready to slug someone.

"Crap, dudes, we should just have stopped at the House of Pizza," says Tommie wistfully, thinking to himself that God can't be all bad, as long as there is pizza in the world. Avril Cheyenne, with a pizza? He can't imagine anything better. God would be perfect, the Cause being at least as great as the Effect. But he doesn't think that far. He just feels it.

There is a lull in the conversation as they slog their way up out of the river valley. They top the ridge at Long Lane and continue straight ahead on Stehman Road.

"Time for a whizz," says Tommie, jogging off the side of the road.

"Yeah," says Harlan. All three forage for a location in the cornfield on the west side of the country lane. Soon, they're stumbling back onto the narrow road, down into the next valley.

"Ferris, could you decide to stop believing in God?" asks Harlan, back with the seemingly interminable thread of inquiry. No attention deficit here. His deficit is too much attention. "I mean, is it really up to you? Don't you simply recognize or acknowledge what to you seems to be the case? You don't invent your answer: you live, think, observe, and your conclusion formulates itself. It's almost like math. You can only recognize what you believe to be the case, you can't simply invent an answer that deviates from all of your own perceived evidence."

Tommie and Ferris both ruminated on this in spite of themselves, wondering what the hell Harlan was talking about, and if it had any remote connection to gayness, asparagus, pizza, or God.

"How much of what you believe is really up to you?" continued Harlan, oblivious to the silence. "Maybe we'd like to believe that we're in charge of our beliefs, but maybe we simply must accept what we perceive to be the case, whether we like it or not. For example, I may want to believe that people are basically good and that nobody would actually hurt somebody just for the hell of it, but that isn't exactly how I perceive humanity. To me, people don't seem basically good, and some evil bastards do hurt others just for the hell of it. So I have to believe something that I don't necessarily choose to believe, if by choosing you mean just deciding what beliefs you would like the most. It's not a belief I actually *like*, but I hold it as true. It's all about acknowledging what *is* the case, not what you *want* to be the case."

"I hold pizza as true, I acknowledge that pizza is the case, and I like pizza," Ferris bellows in between breaths. Ferris does like pizza. He does not like asparagus. And he is not gay. As his feet slap the asphalt, the nearby hills echo.

"Wow, dude. That's deep. Look, just listen to me for a minute. You pretty much have to anyway, losers," said Harlan. Tommie and Ferris exchanged pensive glances but remained silent. "So, let's just say, for the sake of argument, that beliefs are not really voluntary, and neither is gayness. That is, you can choose only to acknowledge your actual beliefs and your gayness or straightness, or you can deny these things, and lie to yourself and others. The essential thing is to face the truth about yourself and your beliefs." Harlan's got his second wind. Maybe he should wait with the verbiage until they get back and put it on YouTube or something, because both of his companion's eyes were glazing over faster than a Christmas ham. They plod forward toward the next ridge, past a farm to their west.

"Watch out! Watch out!" The glaze is gone, at least for Tommie.

A couple of growling farm dogs are fast making their approach to the narrow path that passes for a county road between the homestead and the barn. The east side is fenced, leaving the runners no place to go. They make an effort to sprint up the road, a comical effort, especially since they are tackling a significant grade. Ferris takes the lead as the two dogs get dangerously close to Harlan and Tommie, barking like crazy. The canines are just counting coup. They'd rather go back to the shade of the porch, but they've got to respond to the interlopers or they won't be worth their canine salt.

Tommie is sprinting forward, trying to look back and survail the dogs, all the while yelling like his pants are on fire. Sad. But Harlan doesn't look any better. Only he's got less spandex showing. His arms are flailing and his head is rolling around like he's having some kind of a seizure. Pathetic by any accounting. After a hundred and fifty meters or so, the dogs break it off and turn back for the shade. They trot with an air of triumph. Ferris is fifty meters ahead of Harlan and Tommie, and he's already doubling back to see who's cryin' now.

"*Shooby dooby dooby where the hell would you be?*.... Now look who's gay, you big dorks.

Hah Hah Hah." Ferris has enough wind to sing with glee. For the first time, he's actually glad that he went running today. Harlan and Tommie look back and see the dogs standing in the middle of the road, about seventy-five meters back. One appears to be about forty pounds, a mutt, and at least fifteen years old—old enough to be thinking about doggie hospice. The other dog is a reddish, mutant seventeen-pound or so chihuahua. The runners regroup and try to stop hyperventilating. They continue up the hill in silence. Nobody speaks for a good five minutes. Ferris has the grin of silent satisfaction. They've been out there for over thirty minutes. The amount of remaining glycogen begins to vary inversely with the degree of free association.

Tommie, in spite of himself, is back to thinking about gayness. "Harlan, so you're saying that gay people don't want to be gay, just like you don't want to believe things that you don't like, like people are not basically good? But then, you say that unless you're gay, you can't really know how you would feel about being gay. So, unless you're gay, you can't know that gay people wouldn't want to be gay. You *could* know that you hold a belief that you don't like—that people are not basically good—but you couldn't know if gay people wish they weren't gay. It's got to be one or the other. Either you can know or you can't know."

Holy crap. The pizza is going to taste a whole lot better if we could just stop talking about gayness, thought Ferris. He tries a preemptive strike to end the conversation.

"*Who cares* if gay people like or don't like being gay, you losers? If they like it, they're just perverts. If they don't like it, perfect."

They take a right onto Stoney Lane. It's still a long way to Rock Hill. The Conestoga River meanders through Rock Hill valley. Barring unforeseen incidents, they should make it there in fifteen minutes. The clouds are playing a diminishing part in the blueness all around.

"Perverts? What's that supposed to mean?" asks Harlan, continuing his semiotic exploration.

"How could anybody like being gay unless they were perverted? Liking it would prove you were a pervert," asserts Ferris, whose running form seems to improve with every voiced certitude. Then again, he's still riding high from outsprinting Harlan and Tommie.

"Are gay people choosing to be gay, or choosing to like being gay, after they realized that they were gay, or neither? Did you choose to be straight? Do you like being straight?" asks Harlan. Harlan should speak English for a change, thought Ferris.

"Okay look, Harlan, you pinhead, I don't think being straight is a choice. *Being gay is a choice.* I'm just not gay. I know I'm straight. It's not a matter of liking it or not. It's just a fact. Not that I don't like it. At least, I think I like it. I haven't got much experience, really," says Ferris. "But hey, you guys don't have any experience either, so you don't know what the hell you're talking about either. You just *act* like you know, but you don't have a clue."

"Okay, I don't have a clue. But I can speculate, can't I? I can still think about it. Couldn't it be *exactly the same* for someone who is gay as it is for someone who is straight? Why would it have to be any different? Aren't you just assuming some kind of categorical difference because it's not what *you* have experienced, when in fact it may be a nearly identical parallel experience? Why would the gay person be making a choice to be gay if the straight person isn't making a choice to be straight? Maybe nobody's making a choice," said Harlan, looking back and forth between Tommie and Ferris, who both look like they want him to shut up and run.

They are holding up well after forty-five minutes of hills. They pass through a beautiful forest of oak, hickory, and cedar. Not everything is farmland here, and the diversity of the landscape is a significant part of what gives the undulating terrain its charm.

"I've got a really radical idea, dudes. If you *really want* to know, you could actually talk to a gay person and ask him, or her," says Harlan, after a long silence.

"How do we know they'd tell us the truth, even if they knew it?" Tommie queries.

"Well, if they didn't think that you really wanted to know, that you didn't really want an honest answer, they'd probably bullshit you just to protect themselves. You'd deserve the bullshit."

"You guys deserve chicken shit, wusses. Wusses! And you can pay for the pizza too, since I kicked both of your lame asses back there when the geriatric midget dogs ran out. You guys think way too damn much. No wonder you're chicken shits," bellowed Ferris, almost back in town.

Each runner has hit that precarious homeostasis that arrives just before the precipitous decline into glycogen deprivation and madness. They remain silent as they approach Rock Hill, take a left over the narrow corrugated bridge and ascend the steep hill up to the ridge. The long slog down Rock Hill Road back toward town is pleasant on this now cloudless late summer day. Light winds are blowing from the south and the sun is nearly straight overhead. The smell of sheep and cattle manure is palpable, but all remain silent, as if in meditation.

They pass Owl Bridge Road on their left, a beacon of impending civilization. Walnut Hill Road exudes its silent, timeless beauty as they flow into the borough. They are thinking about running. Tommie looks to his left and sees Ferris. To his right, he sees Harlan. They all make eye contact.

"Why?" says Tommie, acting out his role in the prescribed, well-rehearsed ritual that gives justification to their arduous recreation, a role he has performed dozens of times on countless, long forgotten runs.

"Because we love it!" the three bark together.

7

A PSYCHOTROPIC IN EVERY POT

Is everyone in this goddamn school on *Zoeschliessen*? Is every fucking kid taking some kind of mind altering antidepressant? WTF? Monica thought to herself.

Most say she's ugly as hell, but everybody says she's smart. Maybe too smart. Anyway, she wears these godawful fat plastic glasses and she's pretty fat too, with a blotchy, pasty white face. And greasy as hell hair. Probably could lose a good fifty pounds. Maybe more, since half the kids in this school are fat, and Monica is fatter than they are. Oh yeah, she's fatter. She's pasty white, probably because she never goes outside since she's always reading some big ass book or something, or playing a game of chess online with some dork from Kalamazoo or something. She's the only girl on the chess team at school. She's pretty good at it from what they say. I don't really know because I don't play. Chess sounds more boring than watching my little brother pick his nose and wipe the boogers on his pants while he plays Grand Theft Auto V.

Anyway, I feel sorry for Monica and all, just because she'll never be popular. I guess that means I feel sorry for myself too. Okay. Yeah. She won't even get the time of day from all the pretty people. She's pretty much invisible to them. But what do I know? I'm just the loser that sits behind her in Organic Chem. Oh yeah, and

Spanish. I'm such a loser that she doesn't even pay attention to me. Those who refer (very few) to me at all call me "Slice". I don't want to go into it, but it ain't a compliment. Maybe she's not invisible to me 'cause I'm just about invisible to everyone else. 'Nuff said. I'm gonna fade into black.

*   *   *   *   *

Damn. WTF? Son of a bitch. God I'm pissed. Pathetic. Fucking pathetic. *Why the fuck am I on Zoeschliessen?* The goddamn psychiatrist doesn't know me. That bitch didn't even *listen* to me during our five-minute meet and greet. Hell, she didn't even *look* at me. But she wrote out the goddamn illegible prescription for ninety twenty milligram capsules—with refills— of the freakin' rat poison. I guess the pharmacist already knew it was for *Zoeschliessen* since he couldn't possibly read that shit on the script. He probably filled like 500 scripts for the shit—just for our school. Oh, yeah, it's freakin' me out, just like Angela Wiggins and all, but I don't feel any less depressed. Now I feel depressed, hopeless, *and* really pissed off. Or just numb. Jesus. Fucked up brain chemistry. No wonder. They feed us about 5000 goddamn chemicals every freakin' day and call it food, and that's just in the school lunch.

Then they get rid of Phys. Ed. and recess, and what do they expect? God this place is so boring. I can't even get away from it in my sleep, 'cause now I'm having the goddamn *Zoeschliessen* dreams.

I'd probably be better off on some street speed. At least they won't lie about it and tell me it's curing my disease. The only thing, I mean the *only* good thing about this goddamn *Zoeschliessen* shit is I'm losing weight. All the girls are depressed now, 'cause they can get *Zoeschliessen* to lose a few. Shit, it works better than anything I've tried. I haven't tried working out. I don't like to sweat. Leave that to the weirdoes on the cross-country team. All the girls are using it. Some even think they are depressed. It's like everybody believes that if you have a problem, it must be some kind of chemical imbalance in your brain. There's so much pressure to take the drugs, it's almost impossible to say no. What happened to our fuckin' AWOL parents? Sell outs to the goddamn military-industrial complex that passes for American civilization. Civilization, my ass.

Okay, not all the girls are using it. Some are on *Woeboze*, or *Excyclosyn*, or *Cronsyrilina*, or *Pompusin*, or *Tyrannex* or *Beauspictin* or *Regurgitix* or whatever else chemical time bomb those soulless corporations can concoct. There's a whole lot of shit out there those drug companies are peddling to us. Our brains are going to be so fucked up it won't even be funny. Everybody'll end up as stupid as—I guess I'd better not say. Might get pumped full of drugs, or put in a straightjacket, or disappeared—or maybe they'll take the easy way out and just drone me to death. So much for freedom of speech. Holy shit. Guess I'd better shut up and only open my mouth long enough to shove down the happy pill.

Yeah, well anyway, Angela Wiggins really freaked out one day in Spanish class. I guess it was a few weeks ago. First she started yelling at Señorita Krais for no reason and then she started crying and yelling and acting real freaky and all. It was kind of scary. Right then I thought to myself: what if she has a gun? She didn't though. She just had a couple of library books, some of the few left in this pathetic stripped down library, and she threw a fat one kind of sidearm at Señorita Krais. Wiggins might have been all freaked out and crazy, but somehow she managed to hit Krais right on the side of her head. The spine knocked her pretty hard and the stupid principal or somebody had to call 911 for the ambulance and it was like we were on lockdown or something like it was Columbine. But it was only the Spanish teacher getting hit in the head with the spine of an Organic Chem book. Shit.

I could learn a hell of a lot more if I just

stayed home and stared at the wall for like eight hours. It'd be a lot safer too. I wouldn't have to be around all these people on drugs. At least Billy Etsweiler didn't throw the book or he'd probably have knocked Krais right out for good. He's got to be 275 pounds, 6'4". Angela Wiggins only knocked her out for a minute or so. It wasn't much to see, but I wouldn't want to get knocked out and fall on the floor and all and get all bruised up by those hard square tile floors or some shit. Nobody moved, except to whip out their phones, take pictures and start texting every cybergawker on this pathetic planet. So much for living in the goddamn moment. Yeah, I know, that ain't so great either.

I think the freakin' drugs induce latent sociopathy so nobody gives a shit about anybody else anymore because they just don't feel connected…to anything. At least that's my theory. If I'm wrong, people are even more fucked up than anyone can imagine. If I'm right, people are even more fucked up than anyone can imagine.

Well, after Angela Wiggins went off on Krais, Jay Ingle the dork started running out of the room and he ran into the doorframe on his way out. He didn't fall down, but it was a set back. He steadied himself, looked back, and watched as a sea of texters transcended the moment by writing about Wiggins and Krais. It's like they weren't even there. They were just...numb, detached, alienated, disaffected. But not depressed. Who the hell are these people? That damn shit must be working! Jay was like the only loser who didn't have a phone, so no wonder he ran out of the room. Well, anyway, this story is boring me so much, to tell you the truth, that tears are coming into my eyes. It's probably the sluicerod *Zoeschliessen*.

The point is that Angela Wiggins started saying that her medication made her freak out. That was her explanation. It was some kind of freakin' antidepressant, who the hell knows what. What a shock. They should just ban the stuff from campus, just like if it were guns. Angela Wiggins was saying that she got all disturbed and stuff right after she started taking the antidepressant, and she got to where she wanted to hurt somebody. She should have hurt somebody that deserved it and not Krais. But it never works out like that.

That's it: the unpredictability of the whole damn thing. I mean, April and Julie and Lorene and Tiffany and Travis and Skylar and Slice and Todd and Casey and Eli and Waylon and Alanna and Kendra were all taking some kind of shit for depression or anxiety or some bogus attention deficit and they were all in fourth period Spanish

II with Señorita Krais when Angela Wiggins went off on her with the books. And that's just the people I know about—and I don't know much. I'm not exactly in the loop. Who knows? Maybe everybody in the whole damn class is on the shit. But most people aren't going around throwing books at people or making a scene. So anybody could say it wasn't the medication. But that doesn't prove anything. All I know is every year it's more people around here that suddenly have a disorder and need that rat poison. The list of side effects they rattle off on late night TV for all that shit is even longer than a whole day at this freakin' school.

By college, we're all going to be a bunch of goddamn mental patients. The first lesson is to accept your illness, and if you don't, you're resisting, which is proof of your illness. Therefore, you must need medication. Blah blah blah blah blah blah blah. Doesn't anybody think around here? Cause this ain't thinking. Get it, **this ain't thinking. This ain't thinking. Wake the fuck up.** This is pure goddamn multinational corporate propaganda. It's the same propaganda shit they feed to the doctors, the same doctors who do nothing but turn a blind eye, go along with the program, and get out the prescription pad. Pretty lucrative deal for those bastards. A real payoff for not thinking, not questioning, not caring. Mother fuckers. Hippocratic Oath my ass.

Get the fuck out of my head. Get the fuck out of Angela Wiggins' head. Get the fuck out of my head. Get the fuck out of pretty much every kid in this school's head. You want to make the world a living hell? Keep on getting out your goddamn prescription pad and writing out scripts for your soul crushing mood altering psychotropics. The bloodsucking drug companies game the system, buy off every elected representative we've got on the whole godforsaken planet, and then peddle their shit to the doctors, after they've suppressed every freakin' independent test result about anything they don't like. If there *are* any independent test results. Son of a bitch.

Might as well take crystal meth. Because this killer medical-industrial complex doesn't give a shit about you or me, and if being **on** the rat poison doesn't kill you, somebody on it will. Since NOT being on it is deviant behavior. At least that's what Arnett Kochenberger said, and he thinks for himself. Come to think of it, thinking for yourself **is** deviant behavior. But don't tell anybody. They might get out the prescription pad.

8

SUREKILL HAVEN

Coach Buffalo Bill's firing up the bus. He's got on his usual fat brown plastic glasses with the strap in the back. He's sporting a new buzz cut, shaved close on the sides. Away meet today at Schuylkill Haven, although some veterans call it Surekill Haven. It's hard not to: the three-mile course is basically up a mountain and back down. The course is so freakin' old that they still run it in miles, not kilometers. The killer mountain. It's torture. That's what cross-country running is all about. No pain, no fun.

We're supposed to be on the bus by 2:45. It leaves at 2:50. One of the girls (or Kenny Zeferino) is always screaming and yelling and running toward the bus at 2:49:55. WAIT! WAIT! WAIT! WAAAIIITT! Usually, the fastest they run is getting *to* the bus, and then they suck something awful in the meet. Buffalo Bill just stares at them with the Buffalo Bill stare like they're holding back progress or something. Every time I'm on that bus, I think that progress would consist of cancelling the meet and going straight to the House of Pizza. But if we tried that, what would we get? Exactly. The Buffalo Bill stare.

I get there early so I don't have to see the Buffalo Bill stare. It's a long ride up to Surekill, something like an hour and fifteen minutes or more, long enough for anyone with sense to reconsider and wonder what the hell they're doing on the cross-country bus on the way to Schuylkill Haven. If there ain't no mountain, we've got to create one. Or drive over an hour to *get* to one. It's just human nature. That probably explains half the crap we humans waste our time on, or more. Well, at least I'm speaking for myself here. I mean, I am on the cross-country team. What more do you need to know?

I see Harlan and Ferris stumble out of the gym door with their athletic bags. I think about Saturday's long run and feel the inner laughter. Next thing I know, they're filing down the aisle in the bus, high fiving everybody until they sit across from me.

"Whus'up Tommie? Ready for Surekill?" Harlan tries to be loose, but everybody knows he's about ready to vomit from nerves. I make sure I sit across the aisle so he doesn't vomit on me. It's okay with me if he vomits on Ferris. Ferris deserves it anyway.

"Ohh yeah, I'm ready to commit suicide so I don't have to run freakin' Surekill mountain," I say, trying to keep it light. "Or jump out the window and run straight to the House of Pizza." I have visions of the horror that unfolded at last year's meet, but that's a different story. I should have quit while I was…behind.

"At least somebody's gonna be behind me,

thank God," says Ferris, with a sigh. Once we get to Surekill, I'm gonna do everything I can to kick his butt, the big loser.

The bus looks pretty full. It looks like we've got just about everybody. I'm thinking it out and counting it up: eight boys on varsity, eight boys on junior varsity, eight girls on varsity, seven girls on junior varsity, and four boys that suck-so-bad-that-they-can't-even-make-junior varsity-but-still-get-to-go-to-the-meet. 35 losers total. Just then, I hear "WAIT! WAIT! WAIT! WAAAIIIT!" Surprise, surprise, surprise, it's Kenny Zeferino. It's got to be 2:49:59.9, since the bus leaves at 2:50. What's he do down there in the locker room, put on make up or what? Buffalo Bill pulls on the handle that opens the bus doors and gives Kenny the Buffalo Bill stare. Kenny is tripping up the step and falls on the bus floor, face down, still gripping his athletic bag. The top of his head hits one of the shiny chrome metal legs on Buffalo Bill's driver's seat with a loud, dull thud. General laughter and mockery. Unwarranted derision. Even some freshmen were bold enough to laugh. Laughter before the inevitable tears, the tears of cross-country. Buffalo Bill's face is still frozen with the Buffalo Bill stare. Nobody seems to care if Zeferino's got brain damage. He manages to crawl back up and slink into the nearest seat.

Sadly, it's right behind Kaitlin Ramsey and Mike Kriddle.

The girls are all segregated in the back, all except for Kaitlin Ramsey. She's in the front row, right behind Buffalo Bill, holding hands with Mike Kriddle. They've got to make a big show of it, since just about nobody else on the whole freakin' bus has a girlfriend or boyfriend and they've got to rub it in. Oh, and they'll probably break up by next week, so they've got to milk it now. Just so they don't do that nasty lip lock right there in the front of the bus. Buffalo Bill won't see it because the mirror doesn't get that row, which is good, 'cause he'd probably drive right off the road if he had a front row seat looking at those losers doing the lip lock. I hope that's not why they're sitting there, so he can't see them. If it is, they'll probably be so dehydrated from losing all that lip locking saliva that they won't even be able to finish the race. Either way, they'll both finish the meet in about five hours, what with the heinous suffering that goes with it, but they still get to hold hands on the bus.

Back when we actually had a traveling squad, they had standards. Now they have five-hour three milers holding hands on the bus, on account of the fact that *everybody* makes the traveling squad. It's hard to know why they're on the team, but I don't think about it too much, like I said, or I'd start wondering why *I'm* on the team and why I'm not holding hands with…well, let's just leave it at that. She's not on the team anyway. She's probably not even on the planet. Probably just a fabrication of some slick marketing campaign. God, I hope not. Where am I going with this? Do I really want to know?

Everybody gets ready for the pain in a different way. A few people have got earphones on, but the music sounds like it's being piped through speakers. One of the girls is playing Pasty Candida. God, help me. Nothing like a little Pasty Candida to get your blood going, and not in a good way. It's Brianna Colby. *"Don't be takin'.…Don't be fakin'.…Gotta keep your love shakin'………… Oh yeah!"* Shut up. That song sucks. Nothing like sonic pollution right before the meet. Brianna will look really beautiful stumbling back down Surekill Mountain in about last place, right after Kevin Klinefelter. If it's *that* loud, she must be deaf already. *"Don't be takin'.…Don't be fakin'.…Gotta keep your love shakin'……… Oh yeah!"* Help, I'm in hell. If there's one sport that proves definitively that humans aren't shakin' it at love, it's got to be cross-country. I mean, if we were shakin' it at love, why the hell are we out here running up Surekill mountain? Unless snot, stench, and sniveling is your idea of shakin' it at love. In that case, you're set.

There's some kind of comic irony here in this whole scene, but not being Harlan, it's probably escaping me. Hunter Frizzell and Caleb Hartshorne are drinking these fat ass cans of some stupid energy drink, just sipping on it like it's going to give them special powers or something. Like the power to run, for example. Believe me, it won't. Those guys are dweeby freshmen. Ferris, Harlan and I pretty much pay attention to them when we need some comic relief and need to torture somebody. They look kinda nervous and real serious-like, like the meet actually means something or something, a look you never see on anybody during school because school just doesn't seem to matter that much.

Cameron Moyer is staring out at the cow dung in the adjacent field, drinking his big ass energy drink. The thing looks like a quart-sized can. Kind of pathetic, Moyer sucking on that big can. Soon he'll be sucking on something else— the Surekill cross-country course. Now's the pre-suck, and then there's the meet-suck, and then there's the post-suck, where he drinks another fatass can of some magical fluid. Meet days are the triple suck—the triune suck, you might say. And if you add up all the dozens of other losers, there's a whole lot of suck going on. It's the loneliness of the long distance runner, right here on the bus. And you don't even have to run for it. It's right there, staring you in the face. I'm wishing I had a big jug of iced tea, but then I'd drink the whole thing and probably get the runs at about the two-mile mark and that would suck even more.

Suddenly, with the inane sounds of Pasty Candida wafting past my bench, Moyer yells out "Ass wipe. Damn." His big ass energy drink is somehow flying out of his hands, into the air. He's spilled it again. This is about the third time in three meets that Moyer dropped his drink on the bus. He's the butterfinger poster boy. A few people laugh but most feel too sorry for him to really to do much of anything. Maybe they don't want him to go into any loser's manic fury, or maybe he just reminds them of themselves. As usual, Moyer is nervous as hell. Hey, but it's not just Moyer. Cross-country is kind of like getting a knife stuck in your thoracic cavity—right at the start of the race—and then you've got to run for sixteen minutes or eighteen minutes or whatever it is, breathing like you're going to explode, and then at the end, you get to pull the knife out. That's about it in a nutshell. Yeah, no wonder it's such a memorable experience. Exactly.

Well, Moyer's bigass monster can starts rolling around under the seats, indiscriminately knocking into the seat posts, or better said, knocking into them precisely according to the laws of physics. On the seventh day, God rested. And He surveyed everything that He had created, and lo, it was pathetic. The can keeps rolling around. By this time, Buffalo Bill hears it and is giving the rearview mirror the Buffalo Bill stare. I hear a crunch as Frizzell stops it with his foot. Liquid squirts out onto the black rubber bus flooring. Another cataclysm averted, if you don't count the nasty sticky bus floor. We arrive at Schuylkill Haven High School parking lot, under the shade of Surekill Mountain. It is 4:05. I'm wondering why I am not on American Idol.

Hypothetically, the meet starts at 4:00, but there's some kind of an interscholastic two-coach coaching summit to give us more time. We're supposed to have thirty minutes to "walk" the course so that the home team doesn't have a distinct advantage, as least not in terms of actually knowing the course. This course is a slam dunk, but what with the coaching summit and all, we have to walk a little up Surekill.

"It's out and back, that's all there is to it. You can't get lost, unless you want to. Okay, runners, it's up and down. You go up one trail, and down another," says the Surekill Coach, a short fat blotchy guy in his late 40s in silver nylon sweats, white velcro shoes and an Agway Feed hat, with obvious conviction. It's out and back and up and down, all at the same time. The clarity is astounding. The Surekill coach is more than eloquent. His name is Bowers or Bowkers or something. I wonder how many times *he's* run the course. That would be the *real* spectator sport: over-the-hill slobs running up Surekill mountain and back down. Probably be a major media event, make it on ESPN, and draw the biggest crowd in the history of cross-country running in North American. Actually *seeing* people suffer would appease some of the sadistic impulses of our fellow citizens. But then again, it may only inflame them. Okay, okay, here's just one more example of me not knowing what the hell I'm talking about. Who knows? Maybe Bowkers would beat me and suddenly I wouldn't like it so much.

"Is the course marked...with flags?" Ferris blurts out. Never assume. Especially with a sport as invisible as this one is. They could probably put the mountain on lock down and we wouldn't know about it until we got helicoptered out by Homeland Security and ended up in Guantanamo.

"Absolutely, runners. I've got the freshmen up there right now putting in the flags." This, in itself, didn't inspire confidence. Freshmen? Do they even *know* the course? "There's a yellow flag up top, at the turnaround. We've got enough blue flags up there on the mountain that even Stevie Wonder couldn't get lost on this course, the finest in the five county area, I might add. Most challenging. Real cross-country, that's for sure," says Bowsers or whatshisname with confidence, pulling on the bill of his hat.

"Who's Stevie Wonder?" whispers the pain in the ass Hartshorn, to nobody in particular.

"He's the blind Michael Jackson," says Ferris, sounding believable for a change.

"Naw, don't listen to him, dudes," says Harlan with a conciliatory smile. "Stevie Wonder ran this course in 11 minutes and 59 seconds last year during the District meet. It was freakin' awesome. Freakin' awesome."

"Wow. No way! That's *under* four minutes a mile. That's…that's amazing…" Hartshorn says, looking like he's going to piss himself.

"Harlan, quit bullshitting. It was 11:49, not 11:59," I say.

"Holy crap. It's going to take me twice that long," says Hartshorne, with a look of astonishment.

"Three times, and that's if you cut the course," says Harlan, like a steel jaw trap.

Our mockumentary is interrupted by Buffalo Bill, trying hard to get us to focus. He remains very polite in spite of our gross insolence and immaturity. We are the last to deserve it.

He begins with the Buffalo Bill stare. Finally, things are approaching what might be called quiet. "Ladies and gentlemen, may I have your attention? Let's focus on why we're here today. Coach Bowers from Schuylkill Haven Consolidated School District has a few words to say, and then we're going to have an escort from Schuylkill Haven to lead us around the course. The gun goes off at 4:40 today, rather than 4:00, so take this into account for our warm up." Well, no shit, since it's already like ten after four. Bowers starts with the usual welcome speech and all, but I am daydreaming through pretty much the whole thing, so I can't tell you much about it. I just figure it was boring. All I remember is him saying for everybody to be respectful and sportsmanlike and don't try to pass anybody after you cross the finish line and are in the finishing chute and stuff like that. Okay, I've heard it all before. Plus, there's barely anything resembling a finishing chute at this place and only a fool would try passing in that measly thing…okay, maybe he has a point. Taking anything for granted is just a mistake waiting to happen.

I'm looking around for the Surekill team but I don't see hardly anybody. I guess like Bowskers said, they're up on the mountain, or warming up or in the locker room or something. It doesn't really matter. I just want to get it over with so that I can get back on the bus and watch Moyers drop another bigass energy drink. But he usually only drops 'em on the way up, not the way back, and there's really no point in drinking the stuff on the way back, unless you want to stay up half the night. I did get a twinge of anxiety when Bowkers or whatever was rattling on because it suddenly occurred to me that maybe I left my racing flats back in my locker. Crap. Now I'll suck even more. It turns out that when I get back to the bus to get my bag, the flats are right there. I do that kind of crap a lot. Nerves.

Anyway, we walk up Surekill with the escorts until we're about out of sight of the coaches, and then our team captain tells them "We've got it" and we go back to do our warm ups. We hadn't walked more than 400 yards. The Surekill escorts look a little confused, but that's their problem. Our team captain is a senior named Bromley Garnet, but everybody calls him "Skip" or "Skippy" or "Skipper". He can run just about anybody into the ground, including himself. This is why he is a cross-country god.

Skip leads the warm-ups on a grass field beside the start. His sunglasses are reflecting something fierce. He is half here, half creatively visualizing his imminent victory. I am creatively visualizing falling over a 175-foot embankment, going "Aaahhhhhhh." I then visualize cadaver dogs finding me eight days later under a pile of leaves and debris, picked over by wolves. They've got to identify me by my dental records. At the Memorial Service, Harlan says that I was an example for everyone. I then wonder if *he* was contemplating suicide or…accidental death.

Damn, I spaced it. We're back on the exercises. I don't know if I've missed half of them or not. It seems like it from where we are in the order. I'm assuming that I've done them on autopilot. I hope I've got autopilot, since it seems to be my preferred flight mode. Maybe I'm not flying at all, but I'm just…in the Matrix? Holy crap, when does this meet start? Will I know? I regain a semblance of consciousness or what passes for consciousness. Harlan is still right there on my left, and Ferris is on my right. I hope I don't look as stupid as either one of them. We're running through a series of stretching exercises, one and two and three and four and…counting out loud as per Buffalo Bill.

The best thing about the warm up exercises is watching the girls stretch, but that's the problem: when you *are* actually stretching, you can't really see much, and especially not the girls, who are usually sequestered somewhere like sixty-seven feet away. What I can see, boys or girls, looks pretty sad. Some look like they're simply flailing around until they can get up off the grass. Others, like Oberholtzer, look really tight-ass serious. Oberholtzer, in particular, looks like he is trying not to crap his pants. I guess that's what being anal-retentive is all about. Does he ever space it? He keeps looking at his watch about every ten seconds, maybe to see if it's still keeping time. I'm watchless, but I'm still keeping time. What the hell does that mean? I have no idea, but it sounded good at the time. Here on terra firma, I'm pretty much still flailing around with the rest of them, watch or no watch. I pretty much always have my cheap ass digital watch on—18 bucks— but the stupid plastic band broke yesterday—like they always do. The watch'll probably keep working for three or four more years and I could go through the hassle of getting a new band like last time, but it'd probably break by track season and the watch would still work for another two or three years. I guess I could make a bold fashion statement and just duct-tape the band. Awesome. God, what the hell, boy do I keep spacing it. Yeah, here we are, still stretching. I think I'm getting tighter by the minute. Immune to stretching. That's it. Maybe I'm just the original tight ass. It's true, my ass always feels tight, even if I stretch for an hour. Well, actually, especially if I stretch for an hour. Immune to stretching—that's what Skip calls it, but he doesn't even *need* to stretch. He still goes off like a rocket and runs 5K in 15 something. I'll never win a meet as long as he's on the team. It's not fair. Of course, I doubt I'll ever win a meet if he's not on the team—unless the whole varsity squad somehow quits and goes out for synchronized swimming. Do they wear tutus under water? is what I want to know. Geez, I'm spacing it again. And here we are. Still on the oh-so-effective hip flexor stretch. And I still can't see the girls. Well, yeah, I can *see* the girls, but it's like they're so far away I might as well be dreaming. One-and-two-and-three-and-four-and….holy crap, my hip flexors are tight.

After what seems like seven light years but is probably more like fifteen minutes of flexibility and agility exercises, we go through a few warm up strides where you run about a hundred yards and gradually accelerate, and then taper off again. It gets you ready to hit it at the starting line. When I start to stumble forward into a run, everything hurts, and I mean everything – quads, glutes, hams, calves, shins, ankles, neck, back, spine, hip flexors, sartorius along its full length. Even my face hurts. And I'm still tight as hell. Everything hurts. I might as well go back and wait on the bus 'till it's all over. Did I already careen off of the 175-foot embankment? The thought crosses my mind. But then, then the meet would have to be... over... and I'm not at the bottom of an embankment being eaten by wolves or possum or chupacabra. At least, I don't think so. Wow, yeah, sometimes I wonder about my sense of reality.

I now actually realize that I *will* be running the race. Or, let's just say that the odds are now very good that I will be *starting* the race. Prior to this moment, I was able to toy with the notion that I was somehow going to magically get out of the race, even though I rode the bus the whole way up here precisely to *run* the race—if you can call it running. As for careening over 175 foot embankments? I should have walked the course. It's 4:32, at least according to Oberholtzer. Thirty minutes and it'll all be over. Thirty minutes and it'll all be over. Thirty minutes and it'll all be over. My new mantra. And I can't even remember my old mantra. No matter what happens, thirty minutes and it'll all be over. And this is comforting? Holy crap, what am I doing here?

We start filing into the school locker rooms to take our final whizzes and get back to the start. Harlan looks like he is going to vomit. Ferris is double-tying, no, triple-tying, no, quadruple-tying his racing flats. They look like clown shoes, like about three sizes too big. Maybe he won't trip over the laces like he did at

Oxford. Sad. He probably should have gone into the witness protection program after that incident, so he could be protected from himself. I sit down on a locker room bench and quickly untie and then quintuple tie each shoe, duct tape my laces down, throw the tape to Ferris, take a tortured whizz, and jog back out with the herd to the start.

"First runner, Pine Manor!" It's Bowpers or whatever. The home coach always designates the starters. It's just customary, since ancient Greece or something, only those Greek dudes ran naked and had really long, cool names like Microphidepelkallistosomos. If we ran naked, I can almost guarantee that all of the league records would be shattered, if only out of shame and horror. Whatever works. Barring nudity, maybe we should just adopt Greek names. I think mine'll be Sisyphus. Bromley "Skip" Garnet steps up to the line, toeing the line with his right foot. He's about five feet, ten inches, 155 pounds, black long tousled hair, with an excellent tan and shades like Adrien Brody wore in *Dharjheeling Express*. He looks like he is going to kill it. He's not only the fastest cross-country runner at the school, he's, like I said before, also the team captain, piloting our not-too-seaworthy ship over some rough seas indeed (last week was its own typhoon). I'd be happy to be captain of my own kayak. But I'm still creatively visualizing the 175-foot embankment. Damn.

"First runner, Schuylkill Haven." This translucent white dude walks up to the line, says "Good luck" to Skippy and toes the line. He's got a red afro. They shake hands as Skip says "Good luck" to translucent boy. He's about five feet, five inches with skin that apparently hasn't seen the sun until this very moment. He can't be more than 108 pounds. He's suffering from a dreaded incurable condition: no-ass-at-all. I'm thinking that I'll have the privilege of seeing his no-ass-at-all for all of the two minutes it takes for him to vanish into the brush, only moments prior to my descent into Dante's Seventh Circle of Hell, or rather, the 175-foot embankment. Buffalo Bill briefed us on all these guys—he keeps meticulous records, I have no idea why, but they're stupendous—and I know translucent dude is a hot shot. His name is Sorrell. Maybe he just rolls back down the mountain instead of running, saving seventy-eight seconds and setting the course record. Would it be possible? I try to creatively visualize it, but it's hard when I haven't walked the course. All I see is the embankment. It is muddy, the trail slopes precariously toward the cliff....

"Second runner, Pine Manor" Bowers barks out. I am once again jolted out of my reverie. It's Fabron brother number one, Billy

Fabron. He's usually inseparable from his twin brother Bobby, but in this case, he'll make an exception. Billy's lookin' like he'd rather be playing a video game, or starring in a James Dean movie. You wonder if he's here by court order. He ambles up to the line, mumbling to Skip and translucent boy. His uniform appears to be about seven sizes too large. Will he run right out of it? Why is he here? is what I'm thinking. Come to think of it, I pretty much think that every time somebody steps up to toe the line. I guess you've got to be somewhere. At least we got a free bus ride out of Lancaster County. If they don't hurry up and line up this horse crap of a race, I'm gonna need to take another piss. Okay, we've probably been here at the start for ninety-seven seconds. But my bladder can't tell time, and I've got stress bladder syndrome. Or maybe I'm just yellow. At least I don't have no-ass-at-all. Thank God.

"Second runner, Schuylkill Haven." Bowskers is barking again, like we didn't know what to do. Another anorexic with the dreaded no-ass-at-all comes jogging up to the line. He's another hot shot named Kalman, and he keeps running in place like he's on some kind of a freakin' treadmill. Dude, I hear you, I feel like I'm running in place *after* the gun goes off. I creatively visualize myself with a fifteen-minute head start, and everybody except for me gets twenty-pound leg irons on each leg, and they are all blindfolded. I'm leading the race until minutes after they leave the starting line with their leg weights and blindfolds and all. Then I careen over a 175-foot embankment. DNF: Did Not Finish. Eighty-seven percent of the blindfolded and shackled runners finish the course in a faster time than my finishing time from last year. So much for creative visualization. Maybe I should just give it up. Or I'll just have to start cheating in my creative visualizations, like cutting the course and stuff. Maybe there is hope. But I can't get myself to cheat even then. Sad. I'm a loser even in my imagination. And, of course, with the embankment and all....

"Third runner, Pine Manor." Bobbie Fabron steps up, a double take of Billy Fabron, only .003 percent slower. I don't look anything like either one, and I'm 57.9 percent slower. That's got to be some kind of an omen. I'm wishing I could daydream right through the entire race. I can take the humiliation, but both pain and humiliation? Bobbie looks like he's gonna run in place, just to mock Schuylkill Haven Anorexic Number Two, but he changes his mind after he glances over at Buffalo Bill and sees the incipient Buffalo Bill stare. I start feeling like I'm on a movie set for *Night of the Living Dead*.

"Third runner, Schuylkill Haven".

Everything's starting to blur out on me now. I see another guy with long dark hair stepping up to the line. He looks pretty muscular. This dude I'm certain is Chrysander. Why couldn't some of these guys be sick or injured? At least they don't know who I am, thank God. But, unfortunately, I am not sick or injured.

Fourth runner, Pine Manor." Harlan stumbles up to the line. He looks like he is about to vomit. Skip gives him the "chill dude" look, so Harlan keeps it down. He had a lot more fun on Saturday when those two killer attack dogs chased us on Stehman Road. Now he thinks he's going into his Zen mode to conserve energy, but it just looks like he's gonna pass out. This lining up process goes on for an eternity, but it's probably only about two minutes.

After Bowsers lines up the varsity runners, he instructs the rest of the boys to fall in behind them. Next, he lines up the girls about fifty feet south of the boys. The boys and girls are meant to converge a few hundred yards into the course, just prior to entering the woods. I'm in the second row and there is no third row. I calculate that I will not get trampled, unless by a wild beast approaching me from the rear, or some disoriented moron running in the wrong direction. Not too likely, but you never know. I heard about this guy once who got hit by lightning three times. He was probably a cross-country runner. I'm getting goosebumps but I know I'm not cold, unless you count the cold sweat. I feel the grass through my racing flats. My heart is beating in my ears.

"Runners! On your mark!"

I glance up at the sky. It is nearly cloudless and robin egg blue. Is cross-country just another way to avoid facing the meaninglessness of my own existence? I see a small, billowy cloud drift by slowly. I am ready to beam back to my planet….

"Set…."

9

SISYPHUS HAS GOT IT GOING ON

Crack! The starter has fired the gun. The shot rings out, echoing through the Appalachian Mountains, reverberating into nothingness, the sound of incipient torture and doom. Sixty-eight bodies spring forward, thirty-nine boys and twenty-nine girls. Tommie lurches forward. Even his gastrocnemius hurts, not to mention his sartorius along its full length. Within a minute, the runners are disappearing into the woods at the base of Schuylkill Mountain. Some look like they are already suffering. At the start, which is also the finish, are two coaches, two managers, an injured Schuylkill Haven runner, and no spectators. The glamour has only just begun. The temperature hovers around sixty-one degrees fahrenheit at the base of the mountain. It is only too obvious that nobody gives a crap about cross-country, and yet....

Holy God, why am I out here? God this hurts. I'll just think about the House of Pizza. If I can.

Tommie's start was none too shabby, especially since he's usually in about last place, and today he's got five guys behind him at about 300 meters as they enter the woods. The ascent has begun. The trail is rocky, with some large boulders half submerged along the sides of the path. Smaller, loose rocks are prevalent. The trail is winding, narrow, and amazingly steep. Its width varies from eighteen inches to four feet or so, making passing a matter of skill and timing. It skirts around untold trees, some easily a century old. There are roots to be seen—and unseen—with oak, hickory, and juniper trees fairly thick on either side of the trail. Leaves from autumns past cover the forest floor and a portion of the running trail. Here and there, a dogwood. The sycamores, common at lower elevations, are vanishing. Tommie has no idea where he is in the lineup, but he hears footsteps behind him, so he knows he's not last. The vision quest unfolds. Tommie takes a quick not too svelte glance over his shoulder.

God, at least Klinefelter and some girls are behind me. If I can just hold my position. Man, my lungs are already burning.

It's basically impossible to pass on this trail anyway, he thinks, as his rear foot slips on a few loose pebbles. His pace has already slowed down. His breathing is increasingly labored. He is nearing 800 meters, but he doesn't know this. It feels to him like he is in an infinite time warp.

4:56…4:57…4:58…4:59…**5:00**

minutes… Two people work the mile mark. One shouts out the times as runners pass. It is the first time anybody on the Pine Manor team has a clue about how far they've gone. Sorrell is in the lead as he blows by the mile mark, after having ascended 600 feet, or sixty stories. That five-minute mile is probably worth a 4:20 on the track. This guy seems untouchable, unless somebody starts recruiting Kenyans. He has a short, choppy, powerful stride, with symmetrical, fluid arm action to match. His spine seems straight, his torso erect, with a slight forward lean. He doesn't seem to be breathing at all. Only the sound of footfalls on leaves and terra firma. Nevertheless, Skip Garnet is right there, almost on his shoulder, at 5:02. Kalman and Chrysander are working together, within striking distance, as they pass in 5:08. The Fabron brothers are fifth and sixth, Billy in 5:11, Bobbie 5:12. It is the toughest course in the five county area. Everything is eerily silent, except for some muffled breathing and the sound of rapid, uneven footfalls as the runners dodge obstacles and traverse the wayward path. Somehow, the scene seems primordial, natural, even necessary. A small lacuna and PM's fourth runner Mark Winterfield nears the mile marker, noticeably struggling ... 5:22... 5:23...5:24... **5:25** .... A quick start for Winterfield. The wind seems to pick up as they continue the ascent. The breeze evaporates more and more sweat.

...5:26...5:27...5:28...5:29...**5:30**....Sure kill Number Four, Schuller...**5:31**....Surekill Number Five, Zerphy... **5:32**....Surekill Number

Six, Ziegler, all grind by in a linear pack, focused. Where the heck is Pine Manor's Number Five? Silence in the woods...more silence....

How the heck do you win in this sport, if you can call whatever happens a win? It might make a little bit more sense to relate it to golf, but then again, maybe not. It's basically like golf, only a lot more complicated and not at all the same, except for one key similarity: the lowest score wins. That's right: in cross-country, the lowest team score wins. In a minute, you'll see why runner number five is so important. Each team fields eight runners, but only the top five on each team score points. However, the remaining three runners on each team are very important, because they can displace any of the scoring runners on the opposing team, thus elevating the opposing team's score. Each scoring runner gets points based on his or her finish: sixth place is worth six points, ninth place is worth nine points, and so on. Therefore, the lowest (best) possible score in a cross-country meet would be 15 points (1+2+3+4+5). The highest (worst) possible score is 55 points, which would occur if the opposing team's sixth, seventh, and eighth runners ALL displaced ALL of your runners (who then got 9+10+11+12+13). This would mean that your team couldn't have done any worse—in terms of placing. However, they could always run even slower—and the score would be exactly the same, since they already had the absolute worst possible score. Your runners could take three days to finish the three miles and your score would *still* be 55—since *every one* of the opposing team's runners beat *every one* of your runners.

The closest possible score is 27 to 28. (2+4+5+7+9 = 27 vs. 1+3+6+8+10 = 28). The team with the top runner doesn't necessarily win. It really is a team effort. A tie is not possible, but the entire meet could be won by your last man edging somebody out by one-tenth of one second, so *every step of every runner out there matters*. Here's a hypothetical meet, for example, just so you get the idea, otherwise there's no point in even watching the race:

1. SH #1
2. SH #2
3. SH #3
4. PM #1
5. PM #2
6. PM #3
7. PM #4
8. PM #5
9. PM #6
10. PM #7
11. PM #8
12. SH #4
13. SH #5

14. SH #6
15. SH #7
16. SH #8

In the above example, Surekill has a total of 31 points. Pine Manor has a total of 30 points. Even though Surekill runners took first, second, and third places, they still lost the meet by one point, since their fourth and fifth runners were displaced by Pine Manor's sixth, seventh and eighth runners. Had Surekill's fourth and fifth runners only beaten Pine Manor's eighth, the score would have been 29 to 30 in Surekill's favor. Finish times are irrelevant. Only place matters. So, theoretically, all sixteen runners above could finish within a hair's breadth of one another, or the spread could be fifteen minutes, and the score would be *exactly the same*.

Tactics are very important. Overall time doesn't mean anything if your team can't keep their point total to 27 points or less. And no one *in* the race is privy to all the information necessary to know what the running point total is at any particular time in the race. Each runner must utilize all available skill, cunning, intrigue, speed, tactics and guts to beat as many runners as possible to that distant finish line—and working with one's teammates can make all the difference —especially in terms of breaking the spirit of your opponents, getting them to think about what is behind them instead of what is ahead of them. When this happens, they are already psychologically broken....

5:45...5:46...5:47...**5:48**.... Holy crap, after a sixteen-second gap it's Surekill Number Seven, Shertzer, by himself, pounding his way past the mile... 5:49... 5:50... **5:51**.... UNBELIEVABLE! IT'S HARLAN! PM Number Five. He's twelfth overall. He's looking like Tom Hanks in *Forrest Gump*, the part where Gump makes his transcontinental run. What the heck's he been doing, communing with nature? Okay, it was a sixty-story climb....

Harlan clearly has the runner's build—the ectomorphic, ultra-slim-to-the-point-of-ridiculous scarecrow profile—a real advantage when it comes to running as fast as possible up and down mountains—or any place else for that matter. He's 5'9" and barely over 115-120 pounds. He can float where slower runners just pound. His sprint speed is rather pathetic, but he can keep it up for a long, long time. When Buffalo Bill had him out there at the beginning of outdoor track season in March for the 400 meter time trial, he barely managed a 61.7 and then collapsed on the track in a fog of oxygen debt. He benched a measly 65 pounds in gym, and his arms were quivering like he was possessed.

Ferris is another story. Whatever you think about Harlan, just think the opposite and you've got Ferris. He's a pure mesomorph, 5'7" and very muscular, weighing in at 167 pounds, with a good thirty-five or forty pounds of additional muscle that Harlan could only dream about. Not only has Ferris bench-pressed weights significantly north of 300 pounds and dead lifted 610, he's run 400 meters in 52.7. In gym class last spring, he got the school record for pullups: 26. And when Coach Charles is counting, your form has to be *peerrfect*. But out on the three-mile Schuylkill Haven course, few of these traits count for much.

Tommie is somewhere in between. At 5'11.5", he's the tallest of the three, and weighs in at 154 pounds. With just about zero white fast twitch muscle fibers in his entire body, he managed to fumble through the 400 meter time trial last spring in 62.2, but he is an ecto-mesomorph. Effectively, this means he'll never be great at cross-country—and never be great at anything that requires strength and speed—and he knows it. Benching 180, he's got enough strength to snap Harlan in half, but nobody's going to write home about it. And dead lifting triple Harlan's weight is good, good enough even to top most of the guys on the football team, but not good enough to come close to Ferris (or his brother Sammie, who was up near 500).

Where the heck is the mile mark? I think I'm lost. Something's messed up here. God, does my body hurt. Even my pectorals ache, and they're doing just about nothing. My cheek bones ache. My left pinky finger aches. Beam me back to my planet. Beam me back to my planet. Beam me back to my planet. Man is this painful. I can hardly believe I'm out here. Holy crap. HOLY CRAP! It's Ferris…he's wobbling….

Tommie is gaining precipitously on Ferris, who seems resigned to the fact that approaching footfalls mean that he is going to be passed by some asshole… and the asshole of the moment…

"Tom-mie…Boy…." Ferris gasps. They stumble side by side for a moment on the narrow trail, knocking elbows, a ballet of oafishness.

"Uuff" aspirates Tommie Boy. "Ferris, you wuss."

Tommie's invective serves, as usual, as a real motivator for Ferris, who hangs on with all he's got as Tommie does his ultra-slow-speed pass. He stumbles in front of Ferris and they slog on together. Only 450 more feet of vertical climb and they'll be at the mountaintop turnaround, sucking wind like there's no tomorrow. Luckily, they're not thinking about that now, or Tommie might be looking for the 175-foot embankment….

5:54…   5:55…   5:56…   5:57…

5:58….Surekill Number Eight, Landis, rounds the mile marker, ahead of PM's sixth, seventh, and eighth. Things are not looking so good. But then again, there's a long way to go in this dog and pony show. Landis is thirteenth overall…5:59… SIX MINUTES!... 6:01… 6:02… **6:03**…. The herd tramples through the mile point…. Kenny Zeferino, PM Number Six… **6:04** …. Oberholtzer, PM Number Seven… **6:05**…. Mike Kriddle, hot off the hand-holding with Kaitlin Ramsey, rounds out the PM varsity squad. He's cut ten seconds off, at least, on his first mile, just imagining getting to second base with Kaitlin Ramsey. He'd volunteer to pinch hit, if only he could get a walk. On the other hand, maybe Kriddle's only afraid he's gonna get caught and passed by Kaitlin Ramsey, and then they'd have to break up on account of his fragile male ego. That's probably it: just plain abject fear of shame and humiliation. Scrap that second base stuff.

    … 6:06… 6:07… 6:08… **6:09**…. The junior varsity runners start to claw their way up to the mile marker. A few Surekill guys go by, but as per usual no one is noticing, since JV cross-country is like the invisible box within the invisible box within the invisible universe. Maybe someday, they'll rise to the level of mere invisibility: the varsity squad. But then again, maybe not. The odds are not good. The odds are better that they will either quit, get injured, switch to the debate team, gain seventy-five pounds, get hit by a meteor, or get arrested for meth and go to the infamous juvenile detention center, Barnes Hall. On the other hand, they could become Tibetan Buddhist monks and train for hours in the Himalayas, then run eight-thousand miles in two years on their spiritual odyssey. Or, they may be back here again next year for another year of JV sucking beyond compare. It's a wide open universe.

6:10…6:11…**6:12**….Brian Boxer, PM JV Number One….For a 600 foot vertical climb in 5280 feet, an average grade of 11.36 percent, the farm boy is looking mighty fine. He also has a shot—for the next meet—at mere invisibility. Since he has the PM JV uniform on today, he can't get varsity points even if he wins the meet overall—but he can swap jerseys for the next rodeo.

6:13…**6:14**….Rick Pfeiffer, PM JV Number Two gallops by, with unmistakably varied stride lengths. Some crazy thing he read in Percy Cerutty, that old school Australian coach. Who's to say if it's working, or what that would even mean? He looks patently ridiculous, but that, of course, wouldn't single him out in this race. Might as well just flat out ride a horse, but then he'd miss all the glory and glamour, such as it is, of making it up and down the mountain on his own steam.

6:15...**6:16**....PM JV runner Number Three, Tony Zamato shows up, followed at **6:17** by Johnny Himm, PM JV Number Four. They're helping each other deal with the exigencies of the mountain. There's a lull in what could be described as the action.

Holy crap, I think we're at the mile...the mile...uuufff...why?...why am I out here?...uuff...uuff...uuff...here...uuff...6:24...6:2 5...**6:26**....Man this hurts like hell.

Tommie reaches the 33.33 percent mark. He looks like he is about to stop, but he doesn't. If he did, he would be trashed by Ferris, who is barreling down on him, or rather, holding on to Tommie with his front teeth... Both are leaning a little bit too far forward as they slog up the mountain, and then, a little too far backward, and then, a little too far forward.

6:27...**6:28**....Tommie is PM JV Number Five, Ferris, Number Six.

What the crap am I doing out here? Why are we running up this freakin' mountain? Are they trying to kill us? Where is everybody else? Where the heck is Klinefelter? The girls? If I see any girl in front of me at the end, I quit. My quads are killing me. My achilles tendons are killing me. I'm sucking so much that my breathing sounds like a vacuum cleaner.

Of all the places to be at this moment, why is Tommie at 40.6333 degrees latitude and 76.1583 degrees longitude in a pair of Pine Manor shorts, a singlet, racing flats and a world of pain? Could it be otherwise? Too philosophical, too philosophical, he's says to himself, just focus on the freakin' race, so you don't come in last. Ferris and Tommie slog forth into the next 800 meters, the steepest terrain on the course. Luckily, there are a few switchbacks to take the edge off of the ascent, but at this point, they don't help much.

Tommie should still worry about the girl's race. Kaitlin Ramsey reaches the mile in 7:21 and looks a helluva lot better than Tommie and Ferris did some fifty odd seconds earlier. She's followed by teammates Brianna Colby (7:33), Cathy Carver (7:49), Christine Geist (8:12) and Kelsie Stoltzfus (8:27). Kevin Klinefelter is the last boy through the mile marker, in a smokin' 8:47. The last girl is PM's Haley Garland, in 11:57. At least, the sun doesn't set until 7:54 p.m., so the runners have a good two hours and fifteen minutes to complete the three-mile trek. But at this rate, they might need to start setting up aid stations.

Sorrell is approaching the summit of Schuylkill Mountain, the one and a half mile mark. The total climb, from the starting line at 453 feet, is 1045 feet, to the summit at 1498 feet.

He is alone, except for his own self-transcendence. The ancient mountain beckons to show its beautific vision. A timer awaits his arrival at the peak….

7:36…7:37…**7:38**….He views the panorama below—thousands of acres of forest land, with few reminders that humankind has walked upon this awesome sphere. He transcends time and space in his own self-reflective moment of homeostasis, the moment when the difficulty and pain of the struggle is superseded by the oneness of all things, a moment wherein he now resides, if only for a moment. This is the moment of which Camus speaks in his retelling of the Greek myth, the moment of lucidity when Sisyphus surmounts his fate by recognizing and acknowledging it, not by escaping it—escape being an impossibility. The moment of balance has passed; he has now begun the lengthy descent. Will it be fraught with unimaginable danger and difficulty? Who can foretell the future? To the uninitiated, the mountain shares no secrets.

Skip Garnet is the second to top the mountain, in 7:55. His face, toiling so close to stone, is almost stone itself, echoing Camus' retelling of the ancient plight of the human animal. The quiet is present as an absence. Only the wind and the lonesome song of a whipporwhill. The pain of man is of no concern to these ancient mighty mountains, mountains to whom man is but a recent arrival, an interloper, an invasive species, if you will. Garnet looks like he has devolved thousands of years. He seems almost one with his path as his feet float quickly and unevenly on top of the rough terrain. His focus is sharp, intent. He harbors no ulterior motives. He is going for the kill. It is part of the love of the game. He feels the love.

Soon, Surekill's Kalman grapples to the top (8:02), with teammate Chrysander drafting close behind (8:04). On their heels are Pine Manor's Billy and Bobby Fabron in 8:06 and 8:07, running strong, not ready to give up any ground. The four fly over the summit and into a reckless descent. Schuler crests all alone, in 8:21, Surekill's fourth man. His eyes, red with sweat, are blazing. The sound of a woodpecker is echoing over Schuylkill mountain. At 8:38, Harlan crests the summit, face contorted, teeth clenched, clawing like Emil Zatopek. He's thinking of his idol, Steve Prefontaine. Like Steve, he may just lose his lunch before this gig is over.

Harlan has moved up to PM Number Four, and he ain't givin' back any ground—or so he thinks to himself in a burst of oxygen-deprived delusional inspiration. Surekill's Landis arrives next, in 8:42, rounding out their top five, followed in short order at 8:48 by PM Number Five, Winterfield, struggling like a mule pulling a two ton cart of potatoes. Surekill's sixth, seventh, and eighth runners, Shertzer, Zerphy, and Landis struggle to reach the height together, in 8:49, 8:50, and 8:51, respectively.   Their strides show thousands of miles of training and the seasoned brows of those who know what they've gotten themselves into.   They know Winterfield and Harlan are both within striking distance, and they're ready to play their cards on the descent. A red tail hawk flies overhead. So do a half dozen turkey vultures with premonitions of carrion to come. Do they know something we don't?

9:09…9:10…**9:11**….Mike Kriddle is still trying to get to second base…in his mind. He scales the summit, with Oberholtzer (9:13) and Kenny Zeferino (9:14) in close proximity. The varsity runners have all scaled the summit. The   meet still hangs in the balance. The runners go around a yellow flag at the summit, and descend   by   another   trail   that intersects the original trail immediately prior to reemerging at the field at the base of the mountain. So many opportunities to go wrong, so much time….

Holy   crap…have   we   reached   the summit?…or have I just crapped my pants? Or am I hallucinating?

Tommie staggers toward the summit and what he thinks may—or may not—be a mirage… 9:47…9:48…**9:49**….He's halfway in less than ten minutes.

Hallelujah…it's all downhill from here. Why? Because we love it! Now I'm bullshitting myself…whatever works… uuuhhh… UUUfff… 9:57…9:58…**9:59**….

Ferris slogs his sorry ass over the summit and wonders why he joined this godforsaken sport just because Tommie did. Who's sorry now? But if he were home, what would he be doing right now? Wasting time on Facebook? Reading some useless tweets from someone he doesn't like or doesn't know? Okay then, this is the shit. Besides, it's all downhill from here, literally speaking. He crests the summit and nearly dives down the narrow, steep, rocky path.

"Aaaahhhh! Help! Help!" Kaitlin Ramsey, the lead female, stumbles upon a flock of wild turkeys crossing her path, just prior to scaling the peak of Schuylkill mountain. She keeps screaming for a good ten seconds, apparently helping her to climb the last fifty meters. The birds attempt to make their not-so-graceful escape, running zig-zag through the woods, trying not to collide with the myriad trees, looking for an opening for takeoff. A few run back across the trail, only feet from a petrified

Kaitlin Ramsey. These birds are freakin' big—and ugly, and really scary, she thinks to herself. These birds were not meant to fly. As Ramsey staggers, pants and screams, she wonders if women were meant to run. Why couldn't she be back on the bus with hunk Mike Kriddle? She tops the summit in 11:27, followed soon after by Brianna Colby, who has narrowed the gap, in 11:35.

Cameron Moyer and Kevin Klinefelter are now walking in single file up the last 200 meters to the summit...13:46...13:47...**13:48**....They stumble over the top and shuffle into a lifeless half jog on the downside. They are both breathing so loudly that a deaf blackbird could hear them two mountains over, just from the vibrations. It sounds like somebody's gonna crack a sternum. Moyer's pulse is 200; Klinefelter's a lowrider 196. Not necessarily higher than the varsity runners, but Moyer and Klinefelter are averaging a 9:12 mile pace. Long after the varsity boys have got their sweats back on, Haley Garland chugs up to the summit, red as a beet, in 18:34. She's a half-mile behind Moyer and Klinefelter—at the one and a half mile mark. The mountain is hers. She begins the descent with unparalleled solitude. Below, the race is over, but she remains unconcerned.

The downhill scramble that is the second

half of the race is as scary as downhill skiing, without poles, through a forest of thick trees and obstacles. The terrain is rife for an accident, with roots and branches awaiting the unwary runner flying by at breakneck speed. The switchbacks are very tight, with ninety-degree turns in a matter of a half dozen or so feet, with trees right there at the edge of the trail. And there are some significant trailside drops, if one hazards, inadvertently, to leave the trail. Passing another runner, then, becomes a significant pain in the ass—if not a matter of potentially eliminating oneself from the gene pool altogether.

Hoooolllyyyyy…CCCrrraaaapppppppppp…Aaaahhhhhhhh…Aaaaaahhhhh…Gggggggawwwdddd…Aaaahhhhhh!! Tommie is crashing through the thicket, somewhere slightly off the downhill trail. He somehow missed a tight corner and…Aaaahhhh…Ggggaawwwdddd…He trips, stumbles like a projectile, and lands in a pile of brush, some fifty meters off of the trail. It is the moment of reckoning. Is he still conscious? Does he still *want* to be conscious? His body is pumping adrenaline so hard that he jumps straight up out of the brush and starts running, even though he is thoroughly disoriented.

"Shit. Where the hell's the trail? Ferris! Ferris! FERRIS! FERRIS! ANYBODY?"

In a twist of fate, Ferris was crashing by

just then, and from the trail he yelled with whatever meager oxygen he had left. "Tommie! Tommie! Tommie! Over here! Over here!" Tommie heard the yelling and stumbled with a new adrenaline burst toward the sound of Ferris. In a few seconds, he was back on the trail, and Ferris was right in front of him, bobbing his head and shoulders as he negotiated his way down the merciless trail. Tommie sprinted to catch Ferris. "Thanks bro, thanks" he yelled in a rasp. "No problem, bro." Ferris didn't look back. Neither of them wanted to see Kevin Klinefelter or the girls. Even though they were running downhill, at this pace they were in massive oxygen debt, incurred as they ascended, but never repaid. Their powers of discernment were diminished even beyond their normal range. Anything could happen. They could perceive anything. Who knows, even wild turkeys could fly out of their asses. And they knew it.

The race up front was close: closer than Sorrell expected. He flew through the two mile in 9:47, and he thought he would, at this point, be alone with the chipmunk, possum, and the sound of the mountain wind. But Skip Garnet was flying like a freakin' madman, like his legs were made of titanium and Kevlar. He covered the last half mile, with a 450-plus foot drop and numerous switchbacks, in 1:57, giving him a two mile split of 9:52. Sorrell had covered it in 2:10, so his eighteen second lead had been whittled down to five seconds—about 110 feet at a 4:00 minute mile pace, or 36.6 yards. He still had a margin of safety, but he couldn't let up for a second. He knew Garnet would do anything humanly possible to grind him into the dirt, to destroy him and take the race. Sorrell kicked it into overdrive for the final mile. Within seconds of his realization that Garnet was five seconds back, Sorrell had dropped his pace to 4:00. The downward slope was still ten percent plus, so the danger was palpable. No one, no matter how seasoned, could see beneath the endless leaves that covered much of the descending trail.

Thirty seconds back was Surekill runner Number Two, Kalman, in 10:22, followed by Surekill Number Three, Chrysander (10:23), both looking strong and in control. The pace was blistering. Next, Billy and Bobby Fabron flew by in 10:26 and 10:28, Pine Manor's second and third runners. As usual, Billy was .003 percent faster than Bobby. Maybe they had a secret agreement. Anyway, they were working together, just like Kalman and Chrysander, only feet in front of them. Surekill's Number Four, Schuler, was next, in 10:37, and then a baroque concerto of birds could be heard.

Landis, Surekill Number Five was next, in

10:57, having recently overtaken Harlan for eighth overall. Harlan floated by in 10:58, Pine Manor's Number Four runner, followed by Zerphy (Surekill Number Six) in 11:09, Winterfield (PM Number Five) in 11:18, Shertzer (Surekill Number Seven) in 11:20, Ziegler (Surekill Number Eight) in 11:21 and Oberholtzer (PM Number Six), who looked at his watch just as the timer read off 11:30, maybe just to see if the earth stood still, or maybe to see if his alarm was going to go off and wake him from this nightmare. Neither happened. He metrically plodded forward down the mellifluous path. Rounding out the varsity runners were Pine Manor's Mike Kriddle (11:31) and Kenny "Sweet" Zeferino (11:33).

"Holy crap, skunk! Skunk!" Ferris bounds like a lummox over a large skunk right in the middle of the path. Tommie, right behind, does a few short steps and leaps over it as well. They don't look back. Their minds are racing. If somebody's gonna get sprayed, it's not going to be them. It'll be one of those wussy freshmen, or Klinefelter, or one of the girls. No way to alert them now. Poor bastards. That's what they get when they run cross-country. Should have stayed home and watched videos on YouTube. What's gonna be next? A rhinoceros?

This is freakin' ridiculous…some kind of sado-masochistic torture that passes for a sport...maybe it's time for stamp and coin club.... "UUFFF...UUUFFF!

Tommie's reverie is interrupted by the sound of a thud: Ferris hitting the ground, right in front of him, and the attendant UUFFF. Apparently, Ferris tripped over one big fat log that was across the path, something Tommie barely managed to clear himself. Ferris sprang back up and onto the trail, almost even with Tommie. Tommie glanced over at Ferris. He had dirt all over his jersey, hands, and face. Tommie almost laughed out loud.

"Why don't you lead for awhile, sphincter? Ferris coughed out.

"Okay." Tommie was still stifling the laughter, even while he was in serious pain. He maneuvered in front of Ferris, and watched for the next log like a hawk. Just then, they rounded a Sharp curve... 12:36 ...12:37... **12:38...12:39** ....Tommie and Ferris loped by the two-mile marker. Meanwhile, the race at the front was. really heating up.

With 800 meters to go, Sorrell is leading by twenty meters, or three seconds. Garnet looks like a giant coming up behind him, pounding furiously down the mountain, sticks crunching in his wake. Sorrell's red afro is bobbing, like a carrot on a stick. The time is just under 12 minutes. With forty-nine second quarter mile speed, Skip will be hard to beat in a dead sprint, and it looks like it might come down to that on the final 300 meter field at the base of the mountain. Sorrell looks superhuman and doesn't show signs of strain, but his lead is still consistently narrowing. Does he have an ace up his sleeve? Finally, Sorrell and Garnet emerge from the mountain onto the field, two silhouettes alone. Sorrell's lead is now on the order of seven or eight meters. As soon as they emerge on the field and the ground is flat and open, Skip unleashes a blistering kick, almost like he's put it on turbocharge. He catches Sorrell half way across the field, with 150 meters to go.

Sorrell can't respond in kind, but he does show increasing forward motion as he rises onto the balls of his feet and pumps his arms with increasing power. Skip carves out a three meter lead, but with only seventy-five meters to go, he is starting to tie up. Sorrell keeps the locomotive churning, chipping away centimeter by centimeter at Garnet's fragile lead. It is almost as if time has stopped. With fifty meters to go, Sorrell is a meter behind Garnet, and Garnet is hurting badly. Sorrell keeps the pressure on, with little change in his form or demeanor. Does Sorrell have time to catch Garnet? The race will be over in less than five seconds…twenty-five meters to go….Skip is still leading by a foot, maybe sixteen inches.

Sorrell is still poker faced, but clearly straining with everything he's got. Skip reaches the line, diving, as Sorrell leans and lunges. Their chests touch the finish tape together, and they go down onto the turf together. The time is 14:02.6. 4:40.8 per mile. Awesome.

Chrysander, Kalman, and Schuler, all of Surekill, muscle it in for third (14:32), fourth (14:34) and fifth (14:57) making it look like Pine Manor doesn't have a chance. Harlan kicked some mighty ass and moved up to sixth overall, placing second for PM in 15:18. After quite a bit of additional stumbling, Tommie and Ferris finished 26th and 27th overall, in 17:48 and 17:59. Save Skip Garnet, Ferris's final 300 meter sprint across the field was the fastest of the day. Neither was beaten by Kevin Klinefelter, or any girls, so they did not have to join the witness protection program. Here are partial final results:

1. Sorrell, SH	14:02.6
2 .Garnet, PM	14:02.6
3. Chrysander, SH	14:32
4. Kalman, SH	14:34
5. Schuler, SH	14:57
6. Harlan, PM	15:18
7. Billy Fabron, PM	15:26

8. Landis, SH	15:27
9. Bobby Fabron, PM	15:28
10. Zerphy, SH	15:29
11. Shertzer, SH	15:59
12. Ziegler, SH	16:01
13. Winterfield, PM	16:03
14. Kenny Zeferino, PM	16:05
15. Oberholtzer, PM	16:12
16. Mike Kriddle, PM	16:21
26. Tommie, PM	17:48
27. Ferris, PM	17:59
33. Kaitlin Ramsey, PM	20:46
34. Brianna Colby, PM	20:51
40. Christine Geist, PM	23:03
42. Cathy Carver, PM	23:11
49. Kelsie Stoltzfus, PM	24:07
60. Cameron Moyer, PM	26:01
61. Kevin Klinefelter, PM	26:06
68. Haley Garland, PM	32:30 – last

finisher.

Final Score, Boy's Varsity Race =
Schuylkill Haven 1, 3, 4, 5, 8 = 21
Pine Manor   1, 6, 7, 9, 13 = 36

Final Score, Girl's Varsity Race =
Schuylkill Haven 1, 2, 5, 6, 7 = 21

Pine Manor   3, 4, 8, 9, 10   = 34

The bus ride home was quiet as the grave. Cameron Moyer did not drop any big ass drinks on the floor. Brianna Colby did not play Pasty Candida. But Mike Kriddle and Kaitlin Ramsey did do a little covert lip locking—in the back of the bus. No one got the Buffalo Bill stare. The glamour was over, at least for today.

10

TOGETHERNESS

Tommie scans the entire Café de Ville. He wouldn't normally set foot in a place like this, but he's picking up a Large Kissing Gourami Cappuccino for his mom, 'cause she's having a bad day. It's right around three corners from their house, and it's the least he could do, what with her crying and whimpering and all. It looks like Dad might get downsized again, which is some kind of euphemism for the big bloodless corporation doesn't give a rat's ass about you even if you've been working there for your whole goddamn life. But maybe he won't. They didn't say for sure.

The place is busy. There could be twenty or twenty-five people here, and there's quite a bit of noise. Tommie scans each table for signs of intelligent life. There are ten tables. There are three people at the pink table, all talking. Tommie realizes that they are not actually talking to each other. Instead, they are each having separate conversations on their respective "mobile devices". Three hooded drinks sit shrouded before their respective devotees. Now that's real togetherness. Three women out on a Saturday afternoon talking together on their cell phones—but not to each other. It's not rude if they're all doing it. They're thirtysomethings, dressed in bright colors, trying to hang on to the vestiges of youth, today sans the strollers. They probably planned this outing for days. He could only imagine it: "I've so looked forward to spending some quality time together!" "Me too!" "It'll be such a treat!" "It's been ages! I'm so dying to catch up!" and other poppycock. Holy crap, do I even know how to order a freakin' drink in this place? thought Tommie.

The purple table, near the west window, was occupied by a couple of college-age kids with fast thumbs. Their heads were buried as they texted the hell out of their phones, as if Princess Di were back from the dead, or Britney Spears broke a nail or something. It may have been a love thing, it was hard to say, or maybe even a love triangle or a love quadrangle, what with all the texting. Two scones sat on the table on a small paper plate, encircled by drinks. Feel the love.

Tommie's eyes panned over to a square guy at another table who looked like an executive for an office products company. He was having a way-too-damn-loud conversation on his priceless cell phone. "I miss you too! Oh, yes, I had a wonderful time, and I plan on doing it again just as soon as I get back from Toledo! What? Uh...I think I'll be here for a coupla more days...no, it shouldn't be past Wednesday, unless the boss says otherwise!...oh, yes, I can't wait to see you either...what?...what?...uh huh...aah...me either...what?...what?.... uh...uh...hmmm...sure I'll come right from the airport... sure... I'll bring *our little secret*, and maybe a bottle of our favorite wine?… Tuesday or Wednesday night would work?…it could be really late, even after 11:00…oh, even if it's *too late* for dinner?…okay…It's never too late?… *ohhh-kaaay*…I'll be there." His voice was somehow less than seductive, although he was trying, but double-timed chick didn't seem to care. So the loud shameless bastard is waiting for some other woman to show up so he can two-time Ms. Toledo. Damn. I love it here, thought Tommie. He was starting to feel the love, or what passed for it.

Tommie's covert pan continued. There was this seventyish couple at the peach table with heavy coats on, lest the temperature drop below fifty-eight degrees. They both had on some high fashion Reazbo sports shoes with double Velcro straps, his gray and hers white. $39.95 at the outlet on Route 30 East. Ten percent AARP discount. Twenty percent AAA discount, combinable with AARP discount. Buy One, Get One fifty percent off Reazbo Outlet Discount, combinable with just about any other shit you could make up, comes to a grand total of $45.30, with sales tax, for two pairs! Damn, let's go the Café de Ville! Two gargantuan lattes with fat-free soy milk, amaretto, and petroleum based whipped cream, with a strawberry cream cheese muffin for her, and a poppy seed muffin for him for only $19.36. Awesome. The woman was speaking into a cell phone, holding it about eight inches from her ear like it was a horseshoe crab or something. The man was staring at a *USA Today* weekend edition that lay on the table.

"That's wonderful, dear!.. she's what?.. what?... bleeding... bleeding?.. .oh... oh... reading!.. .that's wonderful!...did I ever tell you that *you* were reading before nursery school?...it runs in the family...what?...yes, *you* were reading before nursery school...what...ahhh...ah... yes, even before you were potty trained!...."

The man looked at the woman and kind of shook his head slowly from side to side, but after years of training, didn't say a word. "Yes, dear, you were reading at two, I remember it as if it were yesterday!...I gave you *Animal Farm*, and you were reading it when you finally took your first bowel movement!"

"Mary Sue, can you keep your voice down?" The man scowled.

"No, it's true! Yes, Arthur, you are my first born and I remember it distinctly!...what?...you've got to take the dog in for a teeth cleaning?...right now?...what?...oh... I see...well your father says hello...what?... yes, he's fine ...the blood thinners are ...oh, yes...you have to go... we love you!.. .say hello to Jeannette for us…love you too…bye…bye…"

The man stared at the paper. He looked embarrassed. Was it Mary Sue? Or possibly adult diapers?

Tommie kept panning and scanning, looking for gold in a pyrite world. He noticed four guys at another table that were frat dudes for sure. Two were hypnotized by their mePadds (a name that seemed to Tommie more fitting for a brand of ultra-narcissistic feminine hygiene products), the hot new little computer that everyone worthy of living in an Ayn Randian world just has to have. Got to be plugged in to whatever it is the cyberkings deem worthy of knowing. And you don't want to miss a thing. So, these guys were fingering their devices, oblivious to the outside world. They kind of looked like Ouija boards, with their fingers moving around mysteriously. Another guy with a three-day buzz and the beard to prove it was texting and mumbling to himself, engrossed in his soliloquy that passed itself off for a duet. The odd man out was staring out onto East Cottage Avenue, fumbling with a packet of raw brown sugar, looking like he was about ready to fall on his sword.

Back in the corner Tommie noticed some business chick with a big leather briefcase. She had some freaky earpiece on and was chatting away about some accounts receivable and why couldn't accounting get it right for once, especially after the Enron debacle and WorldCom and Tyco and Lehman Brothers and Merrill Lynch and Archer Daniels Midland and BP and blah blah blah blah blah. She was drinking some kind of frozen death concoction and eating this four kilo death cookie. Blah blah blah blah blah.

Tommie ordered the Large Kissing Gourami Cappuccino, tendered the $6.17, and sat at a nearby table while the experts did all of their whirling and grinding. He stared out the window and listed to the cacophonous sounds of togetherness, or its simulacra. His mind was somewhere in the middle of Schuylkill Haven mountain when Monica LeBlanc walked in the door. Luckily, he was over by the windows, so he could pretend he hadn't seen her. He looked out the window, hoping she wouldn't notice him. She did, but acted as if she didn't. She ordered a black coffee "with absolutely nothing." I didn't know you could get that here, thought Tommie. Monica sat at a table near the counter, and then carefully looked over around Tommie's general vicinity. Okay, he saw her, and she saw him, and they didn't have the nerve to keep pretending otherwise. She kept scanning around the room.

"Large Kissing Gourami Cappuccino!"

Okay, okay, Tommie thought. He walked

carefully over to Monica's table after he picked up the drink.

"Monica?"

"That would be me."

"Tommie?"

"Uhh, that would be me."

"Well, I'm glad we got *that* out of the way." Monica was a charmer. Tommie was standing about six feet from her table, holding the monster beverage, with his feet kind of toed in. They hadn't really talked or anything before, but they knew each other.

"Have a seat, runner dude." Tommie would rather have run out of the Café de Ville. "I didn't know you drank that fancy stuff." He sat down, slowly, across the table, almost like there might have been a coiled snake on the seat.

"Well, I don't. It's for my mom."

"That's nice of you. I don't think I'd do that for my mom. Okay, maybe sometimes."

"She's... she's kinda having a bad day, so I figured it might help, maybe. Sometimes my brother comes up here, sometimes it's me. You know Sammie, right?" Monica stared at him like she hadn't ever really given Sammie or Tommie a second thought. She changed the topic.

"Everybody in this hellhole is hypnotized by some kind of electronic shit. It's the new addiction. Nobody can actually focus on reality anymore. Reality: it's passé. I think we're the only ones actually talking… to each other."

Monica LeBlanc is the new black, thought Tommie—or maybe just the old black. "Yeah, I noticed that."

"You did? Probably because you weren't on your electronic imaginary friend." Monica realized she wasn't the only one on the outside of the outside.

"No, I don't need to plug in my imaginary friend."

"I guess it runs on batteries, right?"

"Nope.   Eco-friendly.   Green. Sustainable." Tommie was spreading it on thick.

"Wow,   your   imaginary   friend   must be…imaginary." Monica is pretty quick, thought Tommie, but I'm not too sure about those fat plastic glasses.

"You could say so, or you could say my imaginary friend runs on imaginary batteries in a world where resources never run out and GNP always goes up!"

"Shit, you must be a goddamn supply-side economist, psychotic, or have reached Nirvana." Monica gave him a lot of choices.

"Right now, I think I'll go for psychosis."

"Coffee with absolutely nothing!"

Monica's order was up. Tommie stood back up. Monica walked up to retrieve her proletarian beverage, and walked back toward the door. Tommie pushed it open with his free hand, and Monica walked out.

"Good thing I'm not a feminist" she said.

"Uhh, why's that?"

"'Cause that would have pissed me off. Since I'm not a feminist, thanks for opening the door, Tommie...Boy."

"Sure. Anytime. See you at school, Monica."

"Yeah, see you at school."

Tommie watched Monica walk off and then glanced down. It was then that he noticed that his fly was open.

11

BIBLE STUDY

"Who would like to open with a word of prayer?"

It's 7:01 a.m. on a Tuesday morning, Room 101, Pine Manor High School. A circular group of fifteen folding metal chairs, three empty. Six boys and six girls face each other. All but two have brought Bibles. The campus has yet to spring to life.

"I'll do it."

John nods and smiles at Billy Fabron. "Okay, brother Billy, cool."

Heads bow, bodies lean forward, hands together. Silence, except for the buzz of the tubular fluorescent lights overhead. Senior John Raush is the de facto leader, but the group has no official head. A feeling of anticipation is in the air, along with the sense that a dozen people have been only minutes earlier yanked out of REM sleep. The attendant vestiges of the dream state are anything but unwelcome.

"Heavenly Father, we thank you that we could meet here this morning for prayer and Bible study. We ask that you guide us and teach us through your Holy Spirit today, Lord, as we seek to do your will in school and outside of school. We especially ask for strength and power to fulfill your command to us in the great commission in your Gospel of Matthew, Chapter 28, verses 18 through 20. In Jesus' name we pray. Amen." Billy speaks with quiet conviction. There is a veritable chorus of soft "amens".

"Since we've only got about thirty minutes, let's get right into our passage for today, alright? It's the book of First John. It's right after First and Second Peter, if you're confused. Bobby, would you please read First John 2:15–17 for us?

"Sure, John. Hold on a second." Bobby rifles through his well-worn leather-bound Bible and finds the passage.

The door opens and Adele Grosshaus tiptoes in, out of breath, with lipstick smudged on the left side of her chin. She takes the nearest seat, right beside Eunice Pogue, who looks up from her Bible, King James Authorized 1611 Edition, and smiles. "Sorry I'm late," she whispers, almost to herself.

"Do not set your hearts on the…the godless world or anything in it. Anyone who loves the world is a stranger to the Father's love. Everything the world…affords, all that *pan-ders* to the appetites or entices the eyes, all the glamour of its life, springs not from the Father but from the godless world. And that world is passing away with all its *al-lure-ments*, but he who does God's will stands for evermore," Bobby reads in a tentative voice.

"What does "*pan-ders* mean? And *al-lure-ments* too?" Bobby wants to know.

"Uhh, it's kind of like they both mean something that is trying to seduce you or trap you, or misdirect you from your path." opines Courtney Weaver. She transferred in this year as a junior from some school in Kentucky around Louisville, so nobody knows her all that well, but she seems pretty smart and has been coming regularly to the prayer and Bible study group. "Whatever it is looks attractive at the time, but later, you'll regret it."

"Really? That sounds like just about everything I do," says Andie Cooper, thinking out loud.

"Except for our prayer group!" laughs Tosha Monette. "At least you're not doing something you regret on Tuesday mornings from 7:00 to 7:30. There was a lull in the room.

"That's about the only time. Unless I regret being conscious. That happens a lot."

"Thank you for reading the scriptures, Bobby. Kaitlin, would you please read First John 3:13–16?" John doesn't join the existential crisis, trying to keep the short meeting focused.

"Yeah, sure, hold on a second...." She fumbles for the passage, laughing a forced, nervous laugh. She clears her throat. "My brothers, do not be surprised if if...um...the world hates you. We for our part have crossed over from death to life; this we know, because because, ah because…we love our brothers. The man man…um who does not love is still in the realm of death, for everyone who hates his brother is a murderer, and no murderer, um…as you know, um…has eternal life dwelling in him. It is by this that we, um, know what love is: that Christ laid down his life for us. And we um in our turn are bound um to lay down our lives for our brothers." Kaitlin sounds nervous but still reads with a hint of conviction.

"Amen. Thanks, Kaitlin. Brianna, would you please read our final reading, First John 4: 19–21?" John, who has bookmarks at every passage, turns directly to the last selection.

Brianna, sharing a Bible with Jason Lake, squirms in her seat and then sits up straight. "Sssure, yeah." Lake pushes his small Bible into her hands. The text is so small that you'd almost need a magnifying glass to read it. There is more fumbling to turn the thin, onion-skin like pages, pages that always seems to stick together right when it's your turn to read, unless you wet your fingers.

"Ah, we love because…we love God because he first loved us. Those who say 'I love God,' and hate their brothers…or sisters, are liars; ah, for those who do not love a brother or sister whom they have seen, cannot love God whom they have not seen. The commandment we have from him is this: those who love God must love their brothers and sisters also." Sophomore Brianna Stollenwerk is shy, that's for sure, but she makes sure to be counted as one of the faithful. Her diction is excellent.

There is a short silence.

"Did all you slackers fall asleep?" asks Courtney, with a big smile.

"We're meditating on the word of God, which I guess you're not," says Tosha Monette, in a dry voice tinged with sarcasm.

Courtney raises her eyebrows, looking pointedly at Tosha. "Right."

Bobby Fabron gets them back on track: "The message here is that the *only* thing that matters is doing God's will. It's the only right way to go. We *think* we know the right way, but that's a mistake. We need to trust God that He'll guide us. What do you all think?"

"Yeah, that's true Bobby, we've got to stick with God's will. But how do we do it? queries John, looking around the circle.

"It's all about love and loving your neighbor as yourself. God gives you the power," Bobby replies.

"We're supposed to love God, but without loving people, you can't really love God. At least, that's what I got out of it," Brianna almost whispers.

Jason Lake, a relative newcomer, hasn't said much at all in the five or six meetings he's attended. He usually looks perplexed and thoughtful, but rarely dignifies his thought by verbalizing it. This morning, things are different. "What does that *mean*? What *is* love?" he asks. "I mean, it's not exactly...*obvious*...is it?"

"Well, it *comes* from God, so we can't love without God's power," says Caleb Hartshorne, still staring at some passage in First John.

"Yeah, okay, bro, but what *is* it? That's the part I don't get," continued Lake.

"It's the Golden Rule, you know, love your neighbor as yourself. It's not exactly complicated. Jesus didn't try to make it complicated," Zack Garnet offers almost dismissively, like it's all too self-evident to debate. Even if it was self-evident, verbalizing said purported self-evident truth was another matter entirely. And if it was self-evident, wouldn't they all, in the end, agree on the issue? All this remained unclear, as per usual.

Kaitlin Ramsey looked up from her Bible. "You could make um... love into some spiritual thing, but it doesn't seem like that's what's happening here. It's really a concrete thing about actually caring about other people, ya know? Like, um, really treating them like you think is right, not what's good for you and not them." She looked different, somehow, in some undiscernible way, when she wasn't hanging with Mike Kriddle at cross-country practice.

"You mean caring about them *as much as* you care about yourself? Can anyone actually *do* that?" asks Lake, seeming to be a whole new Lake. Or a Lake whose spillway had finally given way.

"Only if God gives you the power," John responded, with a conditional. His authoritative tone made it *sound* like his utterance was a self-evident truth.

"So it's a gift?"

"Yes, it is. So few people seem to want it. They'd rather get caught up in the things of the world. That would be us if we didn't keep praying and studying the Word. We'd get caught up in the things of this world too." John exhaled deeply, looking down at the tile floor in the center of the circle.

Bobby jumped in: "You mean the *al-lure-ments* that *pan-der*?"

Jason didn't seem satisfied. "Well, John, the things of this world aren't all bad, especially if God created them." He's read parts of St. Augustine's *City of God* outside of school. "If God created them, they must be in *some* sense, good."

"Not if they're *al-lure-ments* that *pan-der*!" exclaims Bobby, unquestionably proud of putting two and two together, his impeccable logic evident even to himself. It was unclear whether he was in the midst of a spiritual renaissance, or if he was just riding high from Monday's performance at the triangular meet with Donegal and Manheim Central: fourth overall and only twenty-nine seconds off of winner Skip Garnet—not to mention the two-second unprecedented victory over his brother Billy. That would put Bobby about 1 – 99 vis-á-vis Billy.

"I think it means that you are supposed to love people and God and be good stewards of all the created stuff. If you put the created stuff first, you've got it backwards," says Hartshorne.

"But according to Genesis, everything is created stuff, since God created everything from nothing—*ex nihilo*, so anything you love is created stuff," Lake says, with oceanic wisdom. The Latin set everybody back a few steps, but not for long.

Kaitlin Ramsey jumped in. "Except for God. God didn't create God. God was always there. He is eternal. So you can love God and that's not loving a created being."

"So you're really only supposed to love God and everything else will follow? surmises Lake. "What about loving your neighbor as yourself?"

John Raush brought it back to the most

basic level, skirting thorny and abstract questions of theology: "The cornerstone is love, and it's only possible through a personal relationship with Jesus Christ. There is no other way to tap into God's love." John wants to be a preacher some day. He considers it his calling and he has been preparing for it since the seventh grade.

"Jesus gives us the power, if we ask for it. You've got to ask. Loving others like you do yourself is unnatural, that's why you need supernatural power," Eunice Pogue suggests, finally speaking up.

"Hey, we've only got four or five minutes, so we're gonna have to wrap it up. This was a great discussion, what do you think?" John asks rhetorically, and then goes on: "Prayer requests?"

"John, I would like to pray for homeless people and hungry people and poor people everywhere, that they feel the hand of God."

"Okay, Eunice."

"All the guys and girls on the cross-country team."

"Okay, Kaitlin."

"For Mr. Lebowski's recovery."

"Alright, Caleb."

"For our leaders, that they steer the country right."

"Okay, Zack."

"For peace everywhere, and the end of

wars in Iraq and Afghanistan and Libya."

"Okay, Jason."

"Who wants to end with a word of prayer?" Bobby volunteered to shoulder the responsibility. The fluorescent lights continued to buzz overhead. The twelve bowed their heads and prayed, gave hugs all around, and ran out to homeroom. The 7:40 bell rang seconds later. Just another day in the material world, with its untold pan-der-ings and al-lure-ments.

There were a lot of things at Pine Manor High that weren't so alluring, but the least alluring of all had to be the school lunch. What is that shit? That mystery meat? The only way you're going to know is if you pray about it.

12

LIMP IT IN

This isn't what I expected out of life. I don't know what I expected, but this isn't it. I don't know exactly what possessed me to stumble out of bed and hit the streets, but here I am again. I've got a lot of time to think when I'm out here running early in the morning. Hell, you could *almost* say it's late at night. All I've got is time to think. I must be dedicated. Or just stupid. Or with nothing better to do. Probably all of the above. I keep lowering my expectations—at least, that's what I *think* I'm doing—but no matter how much I lower them, I'm *still* disappointed. Now I'm disappointed because I don't think I can lower them any more. It's like a fustercluck to the nth degree, is what I'd say. And I don't think I'm gonna think my way out of it. Or run my way out of it. That's disappointing too. Everywhere I look, things are rife with disappointment.

It's dark enough, that's for sure, but at least we've got streetlights in town and with my headlamp and all, I can get out here at 5:15. The only way I'm gonna make varsity is to work a lot harder than everybody else on the team, and I mean everybody. Maybe I don't have all the talent in the world, I mean I'm no Meb Keflezighi or Bernard Legat or anything, but I can always get better, so there's always something to shoot for. Besides, once I get my butt out here it's really peaceful in a way, if you know what I mean. It would be great if Sammie were out here too, but I understand he's focused on football and doesn't want to run this long distance stuff. I mean, I wouldn't want to run forty-yard sprints with him in a full uniform with pads either, to tell you the truth. I'm sure I'd be dead last. So, I go down West Charlotte and up North Duke and make this loop through the college and wind back to the house. It's like four miles on the GPS, maybe 32 minutes or so. Basically all in the dark, unless it's summer and in that case I wouldn't be out here so early to start with anyway.

This definitely isn't what I expected, that's true, but I'm not even too sure what I mean, since like I said I didn't know what my expectations were to begin with. I guess I expected I'd be closer to my parents, but they seem like they're in another world, or on another planet. Busy, busy, busy, busy, busy. If they weren't, we wouldn't be living too well, because we're not living that hot right now. Sammie has the job at the House of Pizza, and I had this summer job that didn't amount to much, but that's not worth talking about. I still haven't gotten any kind of a real job. That is, if I can *get* a real job, the way the economy is and all. Sammie said he was gonna put in a word for me, but I haven't heard anything. No wonder I can't get a girlfriend.

The economy? It plain sucks. It used to

be pimply-faced teenagers and old bastards working at all the burger joints around here. Now, I see thirty and forty-year-old men with looks of desperation.

And they're not all losers either. A couple of my friends' parents work in joints like that, and they aren't dumb. When it comes to Mom and Dad, well, Mom and Dad work pretty much eight days a week, so what else can we do? I remember that time Dad came home and was all pissed off because he had to take a pay freeze for the second year in a row, but that was nothing compared to the year *after* that, when he had to take a twenty-five percent pay cut—or he could hit the road. He didn't say anything that year. I think I was in ninth grade.

I found out about it later when Mom was crying. She took another part-time job after that, for like seven cents an hour and I tried to tell her that with gas prices being so freakin' high, she was probably working for free. But I didn't actually tell her that. I think I went up to the Café de Ville and got her a large Kissing Gourami Latte with fat free milk and fake whipped cream, because I knew it was her favorite and she would feel better for about two seconds, and besides, Dad was at work as usual. It was then that I started thinking that if Dad left us, we would probably just think he was working overtime and he'd be in

Tahiti—or dead—for two months before it'd ever dawn on us that he'd gone. Because he's gone now, you might say. He's not here now, he wasn't here when Sammie ran for his first touchdown, or had his first date, or when I wrecked the hell out of my mountain bike and just about damn near shattered my leg, or when I ran my first cross-country race or when Mom had that panic attack and we had to call 911 or even when the tornado sirens went off and we ran like hell over to Mr. McKenzie's house to hide in the basement.

My parents look sad most of the time. It's depressing but true. The whole damn thing is depressing. When they don't look sad, I just figure they're faking it, maybe for our sake, or each other's. It not just sadness, no. I think it's something else... maybe... maybe the look of desperation, the look of a trapped animal, like Kochenberger's beagle in that cage over behind the Lion's Club pool. Yeah, it's more like that.

I'm sure there's a lot more there that I can't see because I just don't have the experience yet. And right now, I don't think I want to *get* the experience. Not if it's gonna suck and I'm gonna have to put on a happy face and put up with it. And that seems sad in itself, at least to me. No wonder Mom went to our family doctor for something to make her feel better, even if it didn't. At least somebody would pretend to listen to her for about two minutes, even if they had to get paid to do it. The added bonus, of course, was the double-edged prescription for those happy pills that worked as well as placebos, that's for sure, for something like 25,000 times the price. Oh, and the price we're talking about isn't monetary. No way. It's more about saving your soul, or, in this case, *not* saving your soul. If she wasn't there before, boy was she ever not there after the pills. She had this empty look in her eyes. Yeah, I know, she kind of had an empty look in her eyes *before* the happy pills and all that, and that's true, but this empty look was different—almost a little scary, but she didn't cry as much after that so I left it alone.

Dad seemed relieved, I guess, so I didn't want to horn in on Mom's equilibrium, even if it was chemically induced. I mean, if more time with Dad would have done it, that wasn't going to happen, so why bother even suggesting something like more human contact? Besides, it's a post-human world. At least, that's what I was thinking at the time, and I guess I'm still thinking it now. It's a post-human world, without any doubt.

Why do I think that? Well, in order to have a human—or humane—world, where people actually *give a shit* about each other, you'd actually need to put people *first*, for example, at work, at school, in everything, instead of having corporations run the world without giving a second thought to how having an adult couple work a combined 112 hours a week just to make ends meet is going to affect them and their children. That is, how the necessity of working those 112 hours is going to decimate their family––just to keep their family together. It's like Yurgis in Upton's Sinclair's *The Jungle*. The only way that extended family could stay together was if it destroyed itself. And that was about a thousand years ago, and yet things haven't really changed, have they?

When we had to read that stuff in Language Arts, I wasn't too down with it, but now I'm glad I did, at least I think so—if becoming more aware of how the system works is actually a good thing. But like Kochenberger's beagle, knowing that you are in a cage may not be an improvement. It might be better *not* to know, if you can't do jack about it. The question, I guess, is whether you can do jack about it, and if you can, what *can* you do? In the post-human world that I've been thinking about, it's all about the investor—the stockholder, or the guy with the capital, this larger-than-life guy who is most likely some rich jackass who would sell his neighbor's kids into slavery if he could profit by it. Probably his own kids too. And these are the sociopaths that drive public policy? Shouldn't they be the ones in the cage like Kochenberger's beagle, and not all the people out there who actually do all the work? Damn. Good thing I'm in the habit of running by myself before dawn, even if the whole thing's kind of a pain in the ass. If I didn't do it, I don't know what would happen, I mean, my mind just wanders off into all kinds of crazy stuff. I guess I could blame it on the running and quit running. Hey, I never thought of that. *Blame it on the running.* I'll have to think about it a little more when I'm…*not running*.

How many adults are on happy pills anyway? Is Dad on them and I just don't know it? He would be way too ashamed to admit it, so if he *was* on them, there's no way Sammie or I would know. Hell, Mom probably wouldn't know. Well, he drinks pretty much now, and smokes too, even though we get on his case about it. Maybe he doesn't need the happy pills if he's got alcohol and nicotine. And I'm thinking about this like it's a good thing? This run must be at least a mile too long. At least.

God, I'm feeling sad. I could go in for some of those happy pills right about now. If I didn't run, I'd probably be taking them, or doing something else that would suck. It seems like my parents just fell for all the shit they tell you about the American dream and the good life and all that crap, and once they got in they couldn't get out. I know they've got too many bills to make any real changes, especially with the mortgage, car payment—on that damn SUV with 152,000 miles on it—and about a bazillion credit cards with $500 here and $763 there. If they looked at it rationally, they'd probably just jump in the hole that the freakin' bloodsucking credit card companies and the stupid mortgage company helped them create for themselves, and that'd be it. Hell, they even got a few left over student loans from like 1983 or something. Half of the debt, at least, came from the crap that *wasn't* covered by insurance when Sammie and Mom were in the hospital. Nothing like kicking you when you are down. They just keep you down and keep on kicking.

So much for common human decency. So much for civility. Civilization is passé. It's all about raping your neighbor as you would be raped if you didn't do the raping first. Okay, that's not really true. When I think about my parents, or Mr. McKenzie, or Mr. Lebowski, or Buffalo Bill, or Harlan's parents, or a whole lot of other people I know, *they* wouldn't do that shit to others. No, they wouldn't. But somehow the *bad* people have got the upper hand, and they ain't backin' down. We're the beagles in the cage. So, like I said, it's a post-human society, even if some humans still live in it.

Where was I going with this? Who

knows? All I know is my parents seem to be working themselves to death and getting *behind* in the process. So much for the college fund. We'll just use that meager sum to pay back taxes to the IRS so we don't end up in some black site in an undisclosed location in Eastern Europe. What am I really learning about democracy? Nothing, apparently, since *we the people* don't really seem to have a voice, not even a whisper. There's no audible whisper of democracy, only a wistful longing. At the rate we're going, surely even that will soon be extinguished. At least, that's how it feels to me. I hope I'm wrong.

I'm learning nothing about democracy because I don't have the *experience* of living in a democracy. If human rights are not the cornerstone of your society, you cannot have a democracy. To ensure human rights, you need an actual, functional bill of rights, not some piece of paper shredded everyday by all three branches of government. Without human rights as the cornerstone, anybody could be shoved into the oven at any time for any reason or no reason. Or hit by an unmanned drone in what passes for an exercise of international justice. It's just that simple.

Unless our leaders are dumb, they've got to know this, so they must *want* it to be this way. It serves their constituents, the 10,000 or so people, give or take a few thousand, who have more than the remaining 300+ million people. That's all I can figure. They must want it this way because it serves their real constituents, and their real constituents sure as hell aren't people who actually have to *work* for a living, or things would be a whole lot different than they are right now. A whole lot different. Let's face it, it sucks. No, you don't see those 10,000 actually working; oh, no, they wouldn't be caught dead answering their own phones, or wiping their own asses. No, in the post-human society, they've got an app for that. It's called slavery by another name. Slavery technically illegal here? No problem. We'll offshore the labor, create international competition, and drive worldwide wages below subsistence level. Then the slaves—the humans—will fight each other over sub-subsistence wage jobs, attack each other over a miniscule slice of the pie, listen to Ben Bimbaugh and Penford Owen Bleck and all those other talking-head asswipe lackeys of the post-human plutocrats for guidance and end up selling themselves down the river. They'll *sell* themselves, that is, if they don't have to *give* themselves away. The post-humans will train them in how to "sell themselves". They'll give lessons on it, since they're experts on it all. After all, commodification really is their business.   Yeah—commodification. At least there's one thing I learned in that Business Practices course that makes some sense. Those post-humans have really commodified the shit out of everything. Now, they're stealing water rights to ancestral village water sources and then selling that same water back to the people in that very village. Now that's commodification. And if they can't pay? Hey, only Satan could have thought this one up.

Holy crap, I'm feeling depressed now, and maybe a little bit angry. What the hell's going on? Running this early really catches me off guard. I'm in some kind of twilight state or something weird. After the initial shock of actually being conscious and stumbling out into the dark, it's relatively painless, but that may be because I go so damn slow that I'd need a bag over my head if it were actually daylight. Racing kind of sucks anyway, compared to just loping along and smelling the wet maple leaves and lilacs and cedars. It's really a nice feeling. It really is. In spite of Oldmensch Suchs and the other parasitic SOB corporations on the planet.

I can't see any way out of the jam my parents are in, other than denial. My mind just feels like it's gonna explode when I think about any other solution. Or, I guess, it just goes around and around, and there's just nothing there. No solution, just a lot of sadness and disappointment and desperation. Being an adult doesn't seem like all that great of a deal. No wonder nobody has a goddamn budget. If you add it up and you're $350 or $550 or $1248 in the hole every month, and you just can't work any more hours without developing some shit-ass cocaine habit, what the hell are you supposed to do? Better not even think about it. Better get some kind of freakin' home equity loan—in the unlikely event that you aren't underwater on your mortgage—or do some jerk off debt consolidation program, or call up one of your Masters, like Fuct Credit Card Services and beg them for more equitable terms at the company store before they turn your life to shit. Yes Masser, yes masser, yes masser, whatever you say masser, whatever you say...

Well, now I'm getting so depressed just thinking about it and wondering what the hell the things we're learning in school have to do with what's really happening out in the real world. I mean, how can KINGDOM PHYLUM CLASS ORDER FAMILY GENUS SPECIES matter to you if your only actual asset just lost half its value and you can't refinance, or your ballbusting interest rate on your Fuct card went up to 29.9 percent, sending you into a death spiral, or you've got medical bills out the wazoo? Mom and Sammie racked up over $30,000 in medical bills, *after insurance*, just last year, and they were both on our same family plan. Some plan. I know for a fact 'cause I saw the stack of bills. The stack that began before Mom even got *home* from the hospital and hasn't stopped since. The stack that's on Dad's desk has got to be four inches tall. That is just beyond ridiculous. A bunch of circling vultures. Mom spent about a week or eight days in the hospital, and Sammie was in overnight for hernia surgery. There was some kind of complication on Sammie, but he's okay now. He's back to his old self—if that's a good thing. I'm kind of biased on that one. These were not elective hospital stays for Mom or Sammie, no way. I guess there are some idiots out there who go for elective hospital stays, but I can't imagine who they are. Anyway, now we're on the disgusting five-year payback plan, cooked up by the death wizards of the health care industry, paying over $510 a month. God forbid if Dad or Mom or Sammie or I get sick *now*. It would put us over the edge, without a doubt. I'm too young to be thinking all this stuff, but the way it is, I'm too old *not* to be thinking all this stuff. Man, that sounds messed up, even to me. Yeah, if one of us gets sick now, it's time to get out the 20 gauge.

It kind of feels like we're all running a 10K cross-country race, but they keep moving the finish line. When you get to 10K, the race is suddenly a 20K, and when you get to 20K, the race is suddenly a 30K. Right now it feels like it is going to be about 10,000K, and none of us are going to live through it. When is the trial going to be over? When does the actual living start? I can see why I might think living starts after I get out of school, but what about Mom and Dad? When do they start living? Dad's 51 and Mom's 48, so when do *they* start? After retirement at 82, four weeks before death?

I'm feeling so sad. Really sad, just thinking and running through the campus, looking at all the brick buildings in the dim light, and all the hopes and dreams they represent and did my parents have those same silent hopes and dreams when they were in college and what happened to them? What did they think they were signing up for? No wonder Mom cries a lot.

The whole thing gives me this really lonely feeling. I can feel the cool wind blowing on the sweat on the back of my neck in what's left of the moonlight and I wonder if this kind of clarity is real or if I'm somehow getting it wrong and they are a lot happier than I think they are but they just don't want to share it with me and Sammie because it isn't really our business anyway and at least they have each other and I feel really lonely 'cause I don't have anybody, never did. I almost feel like I'm going to cry, but I don't. Why am I out here at 5:37 in the morning all by myself anyway, running through the deserted streets, and why isn't anybody else out here? What's the point in running? Is it doing me any good? Am I trying to escape? Is it leading to something and what could it be? So what if I beat Skip Garnet or Sorrell or run the world record marathon of 2:02:59, what does it matter?

I'm feeling this ache in my chest and I know it's not oxygen debt. I'm running pretty damn slow, too slow for oxygen debt. My legs feel just a little bit weak and rubbery. I think it's anguish or something like that about all the stuff I'm thinking and feeling, but I guess I'm better off feeling it out here on the streets because at least the run takes the edge off the pain and maybe gives me a little distance on it. Or maybe not. Anyway, I've got this helpless feeling that time is slipping by so fast and it'll all be over before I know it and we are all just sleepwalking through trying to make ends meet and scraping and scraping and putting it on a credit card and hoping it will all work out, meanwhile we aren't really connecting with anybody. We're just fumbling on through in terror and pain and loneliness: who would choose this?

I'm slogging through campus, flanked on all sides by buildings offering the hope and dream of a higher education, but what does it matter? What difference will it make? What's the point?

What am I learning now at Pine Manor and do I want a bunch more of it? Or is it somehow different in kind here at the university, like I'm gonna get wise and not just learn a bunch of shit I could look up on Wikipedia? What does the higher part really mean? A broader perspective on the world? Won't more awareness—if the education provides even this—simply cause more pain? Is it just about groveling for money, or do we actually have the leisure to think for ourselves? Why think for yourself if you're simply going to be punished for it? Why not give up and get in line? WHY NOT GIVE UP AND GET IN LINE?

Boy, the voice in my head sure is loud. More like a yell, really. Sometimes thinking out here on these pre-dawn runs can be surreal, or downright scary. Damn, my left calf is starting to cramp up. I should've stretched more than two minutes before I ran out the door. I know what Buffalo Bill would say. Oww, a twinge of pain shooting thorough my generally reliable left calf. Limp it in. Limp it in. What about practice this afternoon? Kevin Klinefelter and the whole freakin' girls team'll be kicking my ass. Okay, I'm back to reality. So much for Olympic training and my 12:59 cross-country three-mile. Crap. I'm starting to feel like I want to cry again, but of course I won't. I don't think it's about my left calf, but what do I know? Maybe it's all about my left calf. Maybe I'm just a shallow materialist. There's so much I think I know about from my own experience, but if I would just be honest, I'd have to admit that *even when* things are happening, whatever they are, I often have *no clue* what the heck is going on—in any sense.

It's always a lot easier after the sun comes up and I'm out here with Ferris and Harlan and the other guys and we're joking around and talking about who's gay and who's not gay and who's the biggest dork at school and stuff like that. It's different then because I don't feel like I want to cry and I'm not thinking all about what the buildings mean and does any of this really matter and why I am thinking about all this.

Thirty-four minutes and I'm limping back up the driveway. Mom and Dad are about ready to go back to the salt mines. I can see them in there at the kitchen table eating some awful bowls of cereal, fortified of course with all essential vitamins and minerals, just in case none of them are in the actual food-like product. I realize that once again I'm on the outside looking in, and looking in on something I don't think I want to be in on, but I can't stay outside forever, and besides, there's no other place to go. It's getting a little chilly, what with the breeze and the sweat and all.

I know how much better it will be after school out there running with all the guys, but I still feel like I want to cry. The cramp in my calf is getting a little better, but that still doesn't seem to solve my main problem. Maybe I could just walk it off. I can see the sun just peaking out over the ridge, with a pink glow surrounding it, and I feel a sense of timelessness, a sense of hope, even if I still want to cry. In the still dim light, I limp up the back steps, not quite ready for my 12:59 three-mile.

13

SOCRATES WAS A ROCK STAR
(ENTER THE WINTERZONE)

The classes here are pretty much a waste of everybody's time. At least that's how *I* feel, and it's not just me. Everybody else would tell you the same thing: it's a crummy place if you want to get an education. Walking over to school today, I was thinking the same thought I've been thinking most of the days that I'm walking over to the school: you'd probably do yourself more good if you could just get in a decent forty-five minute nap, rather than stay awake during most of the shit that passes for education around here. Even a *crappy* nap would probably be more beneficial. I mean, it's positively mind numbing. And a numb mind is the last thing you need if you are trying to get an education. Sometimes I learn something *in spite of* the instruction, just by reading some of the classic literature and stuff like that. I mean, I *could* learn something, if I could get around the primary impediment: the "instruction". Hey, *The Jungle* is a case in point. I learned something there. But as far as the "instruction" goes, it's a loser all around. Any kid with half a light on could learn more just by going to the library and reading a couple of hours a day. What passes for "instruction" around here is mainly thinly veiled threats that say, essentially, that if you *don't* pay attention, get in line and do everything we tell you to do (when and how we tell you to do it), your future will turn to shit. It's all about instilling obedience, based on fear. Not a lot there about actually thinking for yourself.

First, they put our minds to sleep, and then they wonder why we aren't motivated to learn a damn thing, unless we're forced to learn if for some asinine test. They make it sound like if you flunk a test, it's a slippery slope, and soon you're going to be flunking tests left and right, and before long you'll be flunking every course known to man—even courses you're not taking—and then, in the blink of an eye, you'll be shut out from every college and every job you could ever have gotten and before long you'll end up homeless, a beggar along the side of Route 462 West, just outside of Columbia, and you'd better not have any kids, because if you do, you'll probably have them out of wedlock and your woman will end up giving birth in a manger. Then your brain will fall out right along-side the manger, which is right there on Route 462 West, and your girlfriend and new kid will have to see it fall out and all. Then a bystander or gawker or former classmate who actually graduated will kick your brain right out into the middle of Route 462 West and a semi going to Wal-Mart fully loaded with shit from China for people who graduated from high school and college and have the purchasing power to buy that crap from China by placing it on their credit cards so that they can pay for it over a lifetime and keep up with the Jones will run right over your brain and it will leave a jelly fish-like ooze all over the highway and it will be seen by your mother, all your relatives, including your third cousin once removed, and all your ex-friends on the Channel Eight News at Five. Your wife will leave you and take the baby, wrapped in swaddling clothes. You will have to move to Siberia and become a ward of the state. The only good part is that you will not know this because your brain will have fallen out.

But you can avoid all that if you just study for the test you don't want to take on subject matter that doesn't interest you in the least— utilizing, of course, your pre-numbed brain, courtesy of all the professional educators teaching you not to think for yourself but to get the hell in line, lest you end up a mendicant along Route 462 West. Terrorism at its finest. Thank you, educators. You've scared the shit out of me about 20,000 times, so many times in fact that I can still feel the lump in my throat and my pulse and respiration are going up just thinking about it. No wonder I always get these feelings of dread as I'm walking over to school. Really, the more I think about it, the more I think it's really *not* the material at all. No, most of the stuff could be interesting—if we were just left alone for like five minutes to do a little discovery without being told what to think and how to think and what's important and what isn't important and what we *should* care about and what we *shouldn't* care about and why we *should* care about what we're supposed to care about and meanwhile we're struggling just to stay awake and not fall out of our chairs and keep from yawning power yawns and looking up at the clock to see if it's almost time for lunch and then we notice it's only twenty 'til which mean we've still got twenty-three freakin' minutes in this fifty-one minute slog and it already seems like fifty-one minutes has gone by but oh no it hasn't, only twenty-eight minutes have gone by and then it's time for the lecture on how we don't care and why when we're older (which we're not) we'll realize how foolish and immature we are now (okay, yeah, what's your point?) and we'll regret not having taken advantage of this once in a lifetime opportunity to learn stuff that we may never be able to take the time to study ever again, and what we're missing by not caring now is so momentous that the effects are literally life changing—and not in a good way—so why don't we just sit up straight, put our feet under the desk in front of us, quit watching the clock and just realize how much we (unknowingly) are inspired by the material (which, in fact, it's *not* the material at all, it's more like the absolutely mind-numbing pre-established, rote "thinking" and "questioning" exercises we are forced to do all during the discussion of what would otherwise be a fantastic piece of reading material and besides, at least half of the people in here couldn't read their way out of a paper bag and they're not going to try either so what's the point unless some boring-as-all-hell "instructor" stands up there and drones on reading it *to* us, which actually happens just about every day now—the days we don't just work silently "on our own"), so as far as being inspired by the material, well, I think we'd first have to *be able to read it*, and to *read it on our own,* and we'd have to be able to read it *without some stupid pre-programmed pedagogical crap force-fed to us* about what it all means so that we can pass some ridiculous end-of-course exam (and everybody knows that if the class sucks on the EOCs the "teacher" could be axed, replaced by another cog who will ensure that regurgitation passes for education). Hell, it's no wonder we're not motivated. See, the teachers have got this mistaken notion that just because *they* bore us, we're not interested in *learning*. Everybody's interested in learning. But sometimes you just have to open the door. As it is now, they are putting us to sleep in droves, numbing us out and catapulting us into what could be a lifelong stupor where learning rarely takes place, and, when it does, it's usually involuntary.

The worst thing about having a pre-numbed brain is when it starts thawing out. *If* it starts to thaw out. That part hurts like a mother, and I'd like to say I'm speaking from experience, rather than some delusional game of mirrors, but I could be wrong. Maybe it feels something like that twenty-two miler I ran alone in minus four degree weather, with the fifteen to twenty-five mile per hour winds. My gloves weren't the best, so my hands froze and went numb. The *real* pain was after I got back to the house. Holy crap. If only I could have run forever, I never would have felt it. A jelly fish-like oozing slime would have been seen on Route 462 West, but it wouldn't have made the Channel Eight News at Five.

Well, all that *was* true about the mind numbing courses, but this year we got this new guy, Winter, who teaches philosophy. He's a doctor, they say, a doctor of philosophy. Whatever that means. I was suspicious at first, as I have been trained to be by all these professional educators, since manipulation seems somehow to pass for education. This being the case, I was asking myself and Harlan and Ferris and Winterfield and a bunch of other guys stuff like: why the hell do we now have philosophy? What the hell is it? If half the poor suckers in this school can't even name the capitol of our own state or do long division, why are they introducing something new to confuse us? Aren't the other subjects more than enough feces to swallow for one four-year death march into the heart of darkness? Supposedly, the state board of education had launched a new teaching initiative, the upshot of which was "entirely new" and was essentially a pilot program to get students to think for themselves. Winter was one of the few new hires in the pilot program. Oh well, they could always dismantle it next year and try giving us our recess back.

That's what my first reaction was, and probably my second and third. But then I got a little philosophical about it, especially since all the other subjects seemed so absolutely repulsive, and I had to sign up for something—in fact, five freakin' one credit courses, minimum, all of them preapproved by the thought police. That, I suppose, would be the school board, state board of education, the administration, or the Wizard of Oz. As far as we lowly serfs are concerned, it pretty much amounts to the same thing.

Now, I don't know about you, but I hadn't the slightest idea about philosophy and what it was and all that crap, but it sounded *cool*, like stuff you don't know about sounds cool and a bunch of cool people were signing up and somebody said it was the second oldest subject in human history after theology, and they didn't offer theology—I don't know why—so I figured, what do I have to lose? It couldn't be worse that Sociology, Psychology, World Cultures, Calculus, Chemistry, Physics, Spanish and all those other thrillers. Well, it *could*, but at least it was different, so I signed up, along with Harlan, Ferris, Skip Garnet, Mark Winterfield, Jason Lake, Kenny Zeferino, Monica LeBlanc and about seven or eight other people that I knew. If it sucked, we could always text message, cyberbully, daydream, doodle, or play video games during class, just like any other class. Maybe it would be like a fifty-one minute recess, and since they took away our real recess, how could that be a bad thing? It couldn't be that much worse than study hall, could it? I hope I don't have to eat my words, but if I do, it wouldn't be the first, second, or 433rd time. Let me just say that I had *no idea* what I was talking about. I couldn't even begin to imagine the real thing. The philosophy class.

When I got there for the first time, third period, Winter was a scary son of a bitch. Big white beard, moustache, side burns, long gray hair, gray vest, pale blue shirt with cuffs, like some forgotten founding father that got locked away in the Allegheny Asylum over on Second Mountain, the guy the history books never told you about because it was just too damn scary, and if you knew, your whole mistaken notion of what the founding fathers were like would be shot to hell. He was maybe six feet tall, big hands and feet, broad shoulders, stocky but definitely not fat, with blue Bette Davis eyes that looked like some kind of secret lasers that could drop planes and helicopters from the sky. I'm not kidding. Holy shit, where'd they get this crazy dude, was what I was thinking. And he looked at me like he *knew* what I was thinking. That was the scariest part.

Or maybe the scariest part was that he actually looked at you at all, so you felt like you needed to escape, but *there was no escape*, unless you could blast through the beige cinder block walls that defined so much of our existence for these four years of eternity. For one thing, he wasn't reading out of a book most of the time, and he sure as hell wasn't using some freakin' CowerPointe slide presentation or showing us some DVD to waste time. He was *walking* around the room, walking right up to people and asking them questions, from like two feet away. Unnerving, to say the least. When I say walking up to people, I mean *right up* to them. Let me be more specific. On the first day of class in August, I shuffled in like everybody else: me, Winterfield, Harlan, Ferris, Zeferino, Lake, a bunch of guys from the team. Oh, and Monica too.

I was hiding in the herd, or so I thought. The last thing I wanted was to stick out. The third period bell rang at 10:07, and I was sitting in my harder-than-cement seat in my chair/desk combo, trying to look inconspicuous, you know, about nineteen inches off the floor, one of those all-in-one chair/desk jobs that make you feel like you're in kindergarten and that you can't adjust even if you're ten feet tall. Oh yeah, and ah, you're not supposed to stick your legs out in front of you either, or on either side of the chair legs in front of you and partially in the aisle, and you really can't stick them under the chair/desk combo in front of you 'cause there's this book rack right there blocking your way, so you've got to keep them like crunched right up to your seat, or try to cram them up in the little space on the book rack on front of you, which works, maybe, if you've got a size six men's shoe, but otherwise you're pretty much SOL. You've just got to suck it up and put your knees way the hell up to your chin. Very conducive to learning, as everything in this environment usually is, and perfect for a cramp in your hamstring or calf, or, worst of all, your ass. It's the ass cramps I hate the most 'cause you can't just get right up and try to walk it off. You're sitting there cramped up like a pretzel in your chair/desk combo and the *last* thing you can do is actually stand up. You've got to prepare for it, so that when the bell rings, you won't try to get out of your seat and fall flat on your face when your ass-cramped half-asleep legs buckle right under you.

At least the combo's got that handy-dandy metal bar book rack under the one piece chair/desk combo. It's handy-dandy if you're sitting behind someone with books on the handy-dandy book rack, 'cause you can just kick 'em right out into outer space, and if you're good enough, they might hit the feet of the person two rows in front of you (a whole four feet or so), and if they go that far, you probably won't be implicated, since the average teacher's learning curve on this kind of crap seems to be about 80 years. Come to think of it, *these* could be the exact same chair/desk one piecers that we actually *had* in kindergarten, with them closing that school and all, and the district wanting to be parsimonious with the educational accouterments like desk/chair combos and such.

Actually, that theory makes a lot of sense. LeRoy Dolan, this dork that graduated a few years back and lives down the street, goes to community college a few miles from here, and he even told me that they have the same chair/desk combos with the harder-than-cement seats over there. He says he's been getting the same ass cramp for the last fifteen years, in his right cheek. If I ever aspire to that particular community college, at least the environment won't be totally unfamiliar.

Where was I going with this? Oh, the scary philosopher dude. Well, anyway, Winter got up real damn close and stuck his left foot, with his big-ass leather boot, right *on* my chair, bent his left knee and leaned in, staring me right in the eyes, his face level with mine, his beard not eighteen inches from my incipient beard. I couldn't jump out of my chair: his foot was there, and it just didn't seem like a good idea. So much for texting, drawing, cyberbullying and all the other stuff I was really looking forward to doing while pretending to pay attention. Okay, I probably wasn't going to do all that. I probably was intending on not doing much of anything, just like any other class. But I couldn't get away with it. Not in the Winterzone.

"What the hell are you doing in this class, Tommie?" he practically yelled. I thought I was feeling an ass cramp coming on. Or maybe it was diarrhea.

"Uuuhhh, uuhh…." A good seven seconds of silence on my end. I was feeling some methane in the lower intestine.

Winter kept his boot up, staring me down. I could feel myself starting to sweat. "Are you saying you don't want to be here, Mr. Carranza?"

"Uuuhh, no," I said lamely, knowing I was about as red as I was ever going to get.

"Then, what the hell are you doing in this class?"

"Aahh, I was interested in checking it out...." That sounded dumb, even to me. But that's all that came to mind.

"That was vague as hell, and evasive. Uninformative in every way, really. You should run for public office. WHY do you want to be here, in *this* class?" His boot was still on my chair/desk combo, and his face was in my space. Normally, I was prepared for any class at Pine Manor pretty much just by showing up. But this was different. Way different.

"I had to take something, and...." I knew I sounded pathetic even as I was speaking. What a loser. Nothing worse than a loser who knows he's a loser. Except maybe for a loser who doesn't know he's a loser. So things could get worse.

"I had to take something...." Winter said with a nasally whine. *"I had to take something...."* he crowed again, even more nasally. He said it with such mockery, I almost laughed, but at the same time, I couldn't believe he was doing it. It just seemed out of bounds. It wasn't just my lower intestine—my entire alimentary canal was cramping up, as well as my ass. Now I could feel the sweat starting to run beneath my t-shirt. This is the once in a lifetime moment nobody wants to have.

"What a pathetic cop out. So, you're NOT saying that you actually *want* to be here, in *this* class. You're NOT even taking any kind of responsibility for your actions. You're simply saying that someone else FORCED you to take *something*, and this seemed like the best of a bad lot, mostly because you didn't take it before so you don't yet know how crappy it's really going to be." He paused, kept staring me down, and then continued. I felt the sweat running down from my armpits and down my forehead onto my eyebrows. "If you CAN'T take responsibility for your actions, you CAN'T be in this class, because philosophy is a subject that DEMANDS personal accountability, personal choice, personal responsibility. If you can't say that YOU have chosen to be here, then you can't be here, because you would be desecrating the very spirit of the subject which we endeavor to study, or, to go further, the subject that we intend to engage in, *as philosophers*." His voice was loud, booming, authoritative and elevating all at the same time, but that doesn't mean I didn't feel like I was about to pass out. Everything I ever said about all the horrible classes here at Pine Manor: I wanted to take it all back. I wanted to be back in any one of those classes, vegetating myself into a nonparticipatory slumber. But it was too late. I'd signed up for the philosophy class. And now here I am, in the hot seat.

Holy crap, Winter was nothing if not longwinded. It sounded like one big run-on sentence to me, almost like I was getting smacked up-side the head. Saying I was *forced* to take the class just sounded pathetic, he was right; and besides, it wasn't true and Winter knew it. Nor was I actually forced to take any of the subjects at this god-forsaken hellhole, so I couldn't say that because, as I said, in addition to making me look pathetic, it wasn't true. I could always opt for the juvenile Penal Farm. So maybe he had a point, to a point. Or maybe he was bamboozling me into submission, and then he was going to put my brain into a coma right before he turned into a fascist dictator. I might take the hocus pocus, brain-on-ice hypnosis in exchange for a 12:59 three mile, or maybe just a little bit of peace and quiet. I thought all of this during an eleven second pause, and then I spoke. Did I have a choice?

"Dr. Winter, sir, I *want* to be in this class. I mean, I have *chosen* to be in this class. I *want* to be here." I almost sounded believable, even to me. I could feel sweat running down my ass-crack.

"No shit! That's more like it, Tommie Man!" Winter grinned, took his boot off of my chair/desk combo, and began walking between the rows. "You *will* be a philosopher, the oracle declares. You *shall* speak the truth and you *will not* be given the Hemlock." Okay, now he's starting to sound freakin' insane, I thought. The Penal Farm started to sound better and better.

"The Hemlock?"

"The Oracle at Delphi has spoken; fail not to heed its words. Fate and freedom become one in the destiny you have *chosen*. But *you* must *choose* your destiny, or neither your fate nor your freedom will be unleashed. The powers will remain in abeyance, as an unwound clock, a heart waiting to fall in love, a rain having yet to fall. You must *choose* the invisible path, and then your *eyes will see* the path you have chosen. Choice and self-creation are one, and you must create without knowing. Truth must be wrested from the tall, silent pines that grow in the dark wood. There is no map to take you there, and you must *choose* both the trees and the journey. In the end, you will reach the ineffable, about which you will remain silent, about which you must remain silent, as Wittgenstein would say." Winter walked an entire 360°, behind every chair/desk combo, and ended in front of the class. He panned and scanned, and then continued speaking. "Any real action, said the famous American theologian Reinhold Niebuhr, is one that *only you* can take. If anyone else *can* take the action that you are about to take, then you are not taking any real action. You are merely deluding yourself. *You must find the action that only you can take.* Otherwise, there is no point in acting at all." Suddenly, his panning and scanning stop and his eyes alight on me, with laser beam precision. "You might as well check out of the gene pool, Tommie. It's self-creation or absence of self, truth or death, a journey toward self-illumination, or a journey toward oblivion. Sitting on the outside, riding it out, that's *nowhere*, dude. And anything that *is* has to be somewhere. Unless you're a *big man, sittin' on his can, takin' a journey to neva neva land....To the truth you be so deaf, gotta go score some crystal meth..."* To my shock, horror, and amazement, Winter had lapsed into a familiar contemporary hip-hop rhyme.

"Madame Xero?" I blurted out. Then I felt really stupid. Harlan was always playing that stuff. I should have waited until *he* blurted something out. Man can I be a dumb ass. Come to think of it, why isn't Harlan saying a damn thing? Or anybody else for that matter? Other than Winter and me, this class hasn't made a sound ever since I've been in the hot seat. I'm afraid to look around. I just keep looking forward, head halfway down toward the desk, cowering.

"You slither down to your homey-town....Bonin' up to gettin' down...." Holy crap, Winter actually knows the song. And this

guy's a fossil. Cool. "How many big men and big women do we have in this room right now, within the sound of my voice?" Silence. "Okay, how many students are sitting here right now? Twenty-seven, give or take one. That's twenty-seven *grande* men and women, or, you might say, men and women who don't exist, who have chosen not to exist." *Grande* men and women? What the hell? This guy is getting his philosophical sermon out of a Madame Xero refrain? At least I can say I was wide awake, even with an ass cramp, an alimentary disturbance of moderate intensity, and sweat running down to my calves. Then, from behind my chair/desk combo, to the east-south-east, a voice crying in the wilderness and refusing to come forth:

"Big man got yourself in a jam....Just about as cooked as a Christmas ham....Why don't you start facin' the fact....That there ain't nobody got your back?" Damn if it wasn't Harlan, that SOB, metrically speaking out the lines. I knew he couldn't shut up for more than two minutes.

"Mr. Harlan! Excellent! An avatar of Vishnu!" Winter exclaimed, flashing his Betty Davis eyes on Harlan, and what's better, *away* from me.

"Aahh...what?" Harlan's triumph was short lived.

"Maybe not, but can you sing it from the

top?"

"Well, I…could…but…I'd prefer not to."

"Nice, Bartleby." The reference escaped him, or so it seemed. Me too, at the time.

"I'd prefer not to, but Tommie would *love* to sing it. His dream is to be on American Idol." That was the biggest pile I've heard since…probably since the last time Harlan spoke two or more consecutive sentences. That knock-kneed skinny bastard with the sunken chest. I'm gonna kick his ass—if I ever live through this fifty-one minute debacle that they call a class.

"Aahhh, T…o…m…m…i…e…B…o…y!" Winter chants, looking right back at me. His visceral tone sure didn't inspire confidence. Things didn't look good at all. "Tommie! Let's hear it! No more silence. Today's your day. Time to blow some hot air through them pipes! Think Susan Boyle!" I faintly remembered some anonymous old British fossil who went hog wild on some singing show on TV, and now people are tripping over themselves trying to download the tune. The only difference was, she actually had talent.

"We've got twenty minutes just to sit here and wait for you to belt it out. Get up here in front of the class." Winter pointed to the floor, right beside him, front and center.

"Are you serious, Dr. Winter?" I was

nearly overcome with a wave of surreality.

"Do I look serious?" He pointed his Rasputin beard at me and simultaneously gouged out my eyes with his Bette Davis lasers. I was longing for Surekill Mountain. Surekill Mountain with a pack of wild boar. There was a good two hours, well, probably more like twenty seconds but it felt like two hours, of interminable silence. I thought I was going to black out. I could feel the sweat running down my neck and right down my spine. I'd rather be on the 135 mile "run" through Death Valley, I thought. How could an introvert get himself into a spot like this? Oh yeah, it was Harlan, that skinny douche bag. Next thing I knew, I found myself standing up and walking to the front of the room, and then turning around to face the Kafkaesque scene. I felt like I was going to black out. Harlan was enjoying it so much, he would have lost his lunch, but he hadn't eaten it yet, nor breakfast, so he simply looked like his oxygen supply had been cut off as he was slowly asphyxiating in the dung-scented Lancaster County air. Ferris too. He looked like this was the laugh of the century. What the hell? I tried not to look at anybody else. Why did they have to offer this new course, and why did I have to be dumb enough to sign up for it? I found myself mumbling the lyrics.

"Big man sittin' on his can...."

"Louder! Start over!" The bane of Winter's bone.

"Big man sittin' on his can...."

"Louder, Tommie Boy, louder!"

"BIG MAN SITTIN' ON HIS CAN... TAKIN' A JOURNEY TO NEVA NEVA LAND...."

"Keep it going, keep it going, Tommie Boy, keep it going!"

"TO THE TRUTH YOU BE SO DEAF... GOTTA GO SCORE SOME CRYSTAL METH...." I had no idea I could sing that loud. It was freakin' loud.

"Ah, yeah, you're nailin' it Tommie! Awesome, Tommie, awesome. Keep it up!" Silence in the room. I decided to dump the self-reflectiveness and just keep belting it out.

"YOU SLITHER DOWN TO YOUR HOMEY-TOWN....BONIN' UP TO GETTING' DOWN....BIG MAN GOT YOURSELF IN A JAM....JUST ABOUT AS COOKED AS A CHRISTMAS HAM....WHY DON'T YOU START FACIN' THE FACT....THAT THERE AIN'T NOBOBY GOT YOUR BACK?...." Silence. I remembered to breathe just as the darkness was closing in around me. Somehow, I managed to remain standing.

After about three eternities and then some, I heard some slow clapping from the back, Southwest quadrant. I hadn't even looked back there. I was afraid to look now.

"Clap...clap...clap...clap..."

I turned my head slowly and shifted my eyes. It was Monica LeBlanc! I involuntarily jerked my head back around fast, before I noticed that she noticed that I was looking at her clapping for me. She's in here too, which makes sense, I guess. I almost forgot she was in here. The Café DeVille seems like another world. Put all the miscreants and outsiders together: or, rather, we'll do that by self-selection, so here we are. Then I heard more clapping, tentative at first, but then even more clapping. Ferris and Harlan, the bastards, were clapping. Zeferino and Lake and Winterfield were clapping. Pretty soon, just about every poor sucker in there was clapping. I started to feel like Susan Boyle, in drag. It was a hell of a victory. I hope I can avoid the paparazzi on the way home.

14

ASS-TRO MAN FROM URANUS

"*Nice singin runr dude.*" It's a text message…from…Monica LeBlanc! What the…? How did she get my number? Here I am in study hall, fumbling around, not wanting to get anything done, not wanting to not get anything done, not wanting to take anything home, which I never do anyway, even if I blow it off in study hall. No matter *how bad* you are, no matter how unprepared, there's always a few schmucks right there—way behind you (unless we're talking about cross-country, and, at least in my case, there's no such guarantee). Hence, no need to do any homework. A text message from Le Blanc. I'm not the king of the text, that's for sure. That's Sammie, not me.

"*Thanks Monica. I guess.*"

"*R U gettin your mom a coffee Sat?*" Why does LeBlanc care? I had no idea.

"*Maybe, I dont know, why?*"

"*Im gonna be by there around 7 pm. Could u meet me?*" Does she want me to get her coffee now too, or coffee for her mom, or what? Does she know something about my mom that I don't know? I was feeling a little suspicious. Are we gonna meet there at the Café de Ville so we can ignore each other and text other people? Then we'd fit right in. Maybe she's there right now. Alright, probably not, since it's early afternoon on Friday. She's probably sleep texting through

Chemistry or something. Maybe she accidentally texted my number.

"*OK Monica. Just no texting, OK?*"

"*Deal, Tommie. C U @ 7.*" Wow, that was the closest to a date that I've gotten in sixteen years, even if it's not with Avril Cheyenne. That was also one of my all-time texting records, for sheer volume. I don't know why, exactly. I just suck with technology. I imagined Monica getting there early. I walk in at seven, trip over the rug at the door, and am catapulted face first on to the hardwood floor, right in front of Monica and a bunch of frat boys and sorority girls all laughing their asses off. Monica spends the evening with me in the ER. I still have plenty of time to text and cancel, tell her I forgot that I had to do something important, but I can't even think of anything right now, so I'll probably have to end up going, tripping over the rug and everything. Damn. Harlan, you bastard. I later found out that Le Blanc asked *Ferris* for my number, so I'll have to get him back later.

* * * * *

Tommie arrives at the Café de Ville early––way early, like forty-five minutes early. He's got on the usual jeans, t-shirt and sweatshirt, with well-worn Asics running shoes. The shoes have faint salt stains all over their nylon exterior, reminders of suffering long and not so long ago. By the look of the soles, this pair has earned its retirement, or, more correctly, its promotion to post-training leisure activity. His oily black hair looks no more disheveled than usual. He sits there and pulls up his quarter socks about twenty-three times as he repeatedly glances toward the door. The place is about half full, which means about twenty people, all of whom have no apparent interest in Tommie. It's like any other normal day: most are enraptured by their portable electronic devices of one sort or another. Maybe they're faking it, so as not to appear alone, or to avoid conversation. Maybe it's a nervous habit. Maybe they can't stop, and what with the new apps, who could?

Whizzing and grinding sounds fill the air as the master drink makers ply their craft, preparing twelve-ounce exotic beverages that cost an hour's work at minimum wage. Tommie checks his wallet at least three times to ensure that he has the $20.00 bill he thought he had. He does. He checks it again later, just to be sure. Sometimes one needs to double check, just in case. He had already checked it a few times before he walked down here. When he checks it again at 6:48, it's still there, with the same dog-eared top left corner, the same blue-inked scribbling about the Village Night Club. He goes to the unisex rest room for the second time. He could be over at Ferris's place, he thought, or listening to music in the basement. Ferris doesn't even know he's here, but he'll find out, given that *he* gave Tommie's number to LeBlanc.

Suddenly Monica walks in, looking distracted, not tripping over the entrance rug. She's wearing a mustard sweater, faded jeans, black boots, and the usual fat plastic glasses. Her dirty blonde hair is as disheveled as Tommie's, with thrice the volume. She appears distracted. For some reason, she looks like a minor delegate at a United Nations summit. Maybe it's the glasses, or the mix of absentmindedness and passion, or neither. It's hard to say. She sees Tommie begin to stand up, and she walks up to his table back in the corner, near the potted plants.

"Hey Tommie Boy, thanks for showing up," she says with a faint smile. She is unusually friendly. She sits down. Tommie sits down.

"Sure. Thank you for showing up."

"You're welcome, but it was my idea."

"True, but you still didn't have to show up."

"Good point, Tommie. I've made the commitment to be here, I want to be here. And now I want to hear you sing another Madame Xero song at the top of your lungs. How about

'Fatty Revolution'?" Was she ever serious? thought Tommie.

"Maybe later…a *lot* later. Do you want a drink, Monica?"

"Sure. What're you getting?"

"Giant hot chocolate, I think."

"Okay, make it two."

"You can hang out at the table and sing 'Fatty Revolution' at the top of your lungs, alright? I'll get the drinks." Tommie Boy carefully negotiated his way between a couple of tables as he walked up to the counter, slowly, so as not to make his earlier creative visualization come true. The twenty-something pierced and tattooed professional behind the counter asked him if he wanted real whipped cream on top, low fat whipped cream on top, fat free whipped cream on top, goat's milk whipped cream on top, no whipped cream on top, cinnamon or no cinnamon, ceramic mug or paper cup, organic turbinado sugar, regular white sugar, clean raw brown sugar, molasses, local organic honey, stevia or equal.

"Equal to what?" queried Tommie.

The white dude with tattoos, infinite piercings and dreadlocks just stared at him. Then he spoke, very slowly. "That's just a corporate packaging slogan, dude. It's probably double-speak for 'unequal'. But then again, unequal could be good too." He stared at Tommie with the dead-eye stare, a little too long and a lot vacuous.

Tommie thought of the pothead stare he got at Pine Manor. "Thanks for the clarification," he said, more confused than ever.

LeBlanc walked up behind him and faced the back of his head. She spoke only to him, in a near-whisper: "You sound confused. Let me do the ordering. It'll be easier. Don't worry."

Tommie didn't move. "Be my guest. I think I need an advanced degree in international relations and geopolitics just to understand the plethora of options. I'm not up to it. I'm going to need therapy just to recover from my inability to order two drinks at the Café de Ville. What the hell's happened to this town? I was just trying to order a couple of hot chocolates. Damn." He turned and faced Monica, who looked like she knew what to do and was going to have no problem doing it.

"I've got it, Tommie." He stepped back as Monica maneuvered straight up to the counter.

The professional was still staring with the dead-eye stare, now affixed upon Monica. "We'll take two behemoth hot chocolates made with triple filtered no chlorine, no fluoride, no heavy metals one-hundred percent distilled Swiss Alps imported European Union approved water, with United Nations-approved fat free no BGH whipped cream, made with cruelty free no war zone Doctors Without Borders verified organic chocolate, each with one shot of World Health Organization-sanctioned organic Peruvian worker's rights ensured espresso, Human Rights Watch designated organic hazelnut syrup, fifty cc per drink, Fair Trade Dalai Lama-designated organic turbinado sugar, non-mechanically ground Amnesty International-approved organic cinnamon, in two green friendly no-BPH no-lead two percent back to the artists ceramic mugs, petroleum free International Sustainable Forestry Association swizzle stir sticks, with one-hundred percent recycled napkins on which to place said beverages."

Tommie was beginning to like Monica LeBlanc more and more all the time. Maybe she wasn't the new black after all, he thought; maybe she was the new red. He had no idea what that meant, but it was in no way dissimilar from other thoughts that flew through his mind on an hourly basis. He laughed to himself. Dreadlocked pierced tattoo broke the dead-eye stare and walked off to prepare the libations.

"Holy crap, how did you come up with all of that?" Tommie near-whispered at the back of Monica's head, laughing. Monica turned around and faced Tommie.

"Practice. I just like to give them shit," she said in a low tone. She smirked and then gave

Tommie what looked to him like a wink, but then he second guessed himself and figured he must have imagined it.

"That was a whole semi-truck load! Nice, very nice. But, that dude is only the messenger, he's not the guy making all the money. He's not making shit. He's probably lucky if he gets a free drink. Look at that freakin' tip jar: there's got to be at least a buck two seventy five in there," Tommie said, as he, with a nonclandestine finger, pointed to a jar conspicuously displayed beside the cash register with an index card taped on, bearing the word "TIPS" in pink highlighter, fancily scripted, with a few little flowers drawn on for good measure.

"That doesn't make any sense, Tommie."

"Exactly. He probably rode his ten year old hardtail mountain bike over here today, just because he couldn't afford a vehicle that actually runs, not because he's some tree hugger. You know he doesn't get anything like benefits, even if he's here for a million years."

Monica was beginning to like Tommie more and more all the time. "Being here a million years could be a benefit in itself," Monica deadpanned.

Tommy started laughing. Even if that didn't make a damn bit of sense, he still thought it was funny. Maybe it was *because* it didn't make a damn bit of sense. "Do you mean here, in the Café de Ville, or on the planet?"

"Well, we'll assume that if you were here in the café, you'd be on the planet, but maybe not. Or, you could be somewhere else, like Pine Manor. That would be a treat. It feels like we've been *there* a million years already. *There* we're gods, because a day feels like a million years. But I was thinking of here."

"Could you imagine the taste of million year old coffee?"

"Stop. Stop. You're going to make my head explode. I can't even imagine the taste of week old coffee. Especially if it's not refrigerated. That's just gross."

"Two behemoth hot chocolates. That's ah...$13.87." 007 Pierced Brosnan was back with the goods. Tommie whipped out his blue with orange trim nylon folding wallet and fumbled for the twenty, got his change, and put a dollar in the tip jar. "Thanks, dude," said the professional.

"Don't be afraid to touch it, Tommie Boy. Oh, wait, forget it, I'll take them back." Monica took the liquid magic back to their still vacant table in the corner beside the potted plants. Tommie closed his wallet, stuffed it into his left front jeans pocket and walked carefully back to the table, lest a hamstring twinge induce a spontaneous fall onto the shiny hardwood floor.

*   *   *   *   *

Now I'm starting to wonder if this was such a good idea. What was I thinking? I mean, I don't really know this guy, well, I've known him since sixth grade, but not really *known* him, if you know what I mean. It's like Lindsay Foley, I've known her for forever, but we don't tell each other what's really going on or anything. We just *know* each other. We're out there to populate visual space for each other, to situate the other in a complex web of shallow social relationships that comprise our ultramodern society. It's just like they were saying in sociology. This shallow web makes us think we are not alone. Well, it doesn't really make *me* think I'm not alone, because even right now I kind of feel alone, except I have this added pressure to actually interact with someone who may or may not care what I have to say and may or may not care how I am doing. So, in some respects, being here with somebody—anybody— is a setback. Yeah, that's right, being with anybody, at least in general, is a setback: something from which you've—I've—got to recover.

This is like the third time in world history I've actually invited someone to hang out with me.

I don't know why I did it. I suppose it's all about risk, but I'm sick and tired of risk. Can't I just get to the place where everything feels okay? 'Cause I'll take just okay. I'm not looking for spectacular. I'm not sure if I'm gonna give up on being friends with all the girls in this town or not, but right now, I don't feel like being friends with any of *them*...I know there's a lot of them I don't know, but I'm not gonna just walk up to them and start talking. They might laugh me down, anyway. It wouldn't be the first time. There've been so many times I lost count in about sixth grade. The laugh-downs hurt like a punch, only they last a lot longer. Maybe even a lifetime. Yeah, why bother when I'm just gonna get another laugh-down? Or it'll be a silent laugh-down and they'll ream me later in their oh-so-goddamn important gossip sessions that go all fucking night—unless they're with some loser of a guy, in which case, they're just collecting evidence to use against *him* later. Of course, they could do that with *any* guy, loser or not. They're probably texting the evidence during their oh-so-goddamn frequent bathroom stops, the ones where the guy thinks they're doing it just for him. You can really sucker a guy with ego. Bitches. Tommie, on the other hand, seems like—I almost hate to think it—a really decent person—whatever the hell that means—and maybe he doesn't say a lot, but he's not a bullshitter and he thinks for himself. At least, that's what it seems like to me, but there's plenty of time to dispel that myth, if I've got it wrong. And I'm often wrong. No wonder I can't trust myself: I'm too rational for that. I still wish I could get the hell out of here. Or, maybe not. God, I hate ambivalence.

Tommie was clued-in to my far-off gaze.

"Monica, are you cool? Don't like the fancy drink? We could go over to my house and I'll mix you up some powdered orange Gatorade if you like."

That's exactly what I like about him. And I don't know what it is.

"Mmmm, good, Tommie Boy, I love my beverage. I'm just thinking." Yeah, I'm thinking all right. I'm thinking about whether I want to get the hell out of here before I say or do something I'm gonna regret. It's almost like he can see it.

"I've noticed. You seem to do that a lot. Is it a hobby or an affliction?" Tommie's distinction is unnerving. Does anybody really *have* a hobby? Yeah, probably so. I just don't get it.

"It used to be a hobby. Now it's more of an affliction." Like consciousness itself, more or less.

"Do you think there's a cure?"

"I don't know yet. Insanity, maybe, or

lobotomy, or chemical lobotomy." Right now I'm thinking about anything that will clamp down on this goddamn insane self-awareness. I mean, how do you get the hell away from your own freakin' consciousness?

"Is it *that* bad?" Tommie asked, with a wry grin.

"Maybe I'm exaggerating, Tommie. Let's just say, I've got a lot on my mind."

"Do you want to talk about it?" Tommie asked with a disarming earnestness, looking me right in the face. The next thing I know I'm feeling a wave of weakness steal over me.

"Yes and no," I say. At least that was probably the truth. Yes and no. And how the hell do you do that? I'm gonna regret it either way. Like every day when I get out of bed. So if that's the case, *it just doesn't matter* what I do.

"Why don't you go with the yes part and see what happens? If it doesn't work out, we can still go over to my place and make powdered Gatorade." He's trying. He's really trying. And it can't be all that easy. It would be a lot easier for him if he were just here by himself. As usual, I'm just a load of dead weight.

"I don't know if it's fair to you to go into it. We could have our nice behemoth hot chocolates and that would be cool in itself." I think I'm already getting too close to the edge.

The pain is seeping in.

"That's absolutely true. Or we could engage in deviant behavior and actually have a conversation here at the Café de Ville instead of talking about whether or not we *should* have a conversation. I mean, that's good too, but we *could* have a conversation rather than—what does Winter call it?—a...a metaconversation."

"That's right Tommie Boy, a metaconversation. A conversation *about* a conversation that lets you remain at a distance and talk while still avoiding a real conversation." That's exactly what I want right now. But I can't tell if it's darkness or light that's grasping the hem of my garment. Why can't I just fade into the big sleep?

"We wouldn't be doing that right now, would we?" He's pretty quick upstairs and I'm sliding down, down to where I can't see a thing. I could tell him I don't feel well and get the hell out of here. Am I starting to feel nervous? Maybe it's just the chocolate. Yeah, right. We're way beyond that. There's a point beyond which you don't want to turn back from the right thing and you can't turn back from the wrong thing. I have no idea which is which. I fumble in broad daylight.

"Yes, I'm doing it, not you. Can I ask you a question, Tommie?" I dive into the opaque black water.

"Well, yeah, I figured that was kinda why we're here and all, unless I was mistaken. We could just talk, and maybe make fun of the other people in the café, like we did the last time we bumped into each other." He's pretty good with people, and I'm not the easiest, and he's good with me. Maybe I should make a beeline for the door. Right now. And get my fucking dead weight out of here. But no, it's too late…I'm going to dive into the darkness.

"Is your life alright? I mean, well…I don't know what I mean. Okay, are you happy, whatever that means? Or, do you feel…okay? You don't have to feel happy, just okay. Do you feel…okay? You don't have to answer if you don't want to." What the hell was that all about, you blubberer? I've got to keep quiet. I've got to. But….

"I can handle it, Monica. Hey, do you have a nickname, I mean one that you will answer to?

I waited for such a long time before I spoke, and there he was, still staring right at me. Tommie looked at me like I was going to say something deep, something revelatory, which wasn't going to be the case at all. "I did have a nickname but I won't answer to it, so I guess the answer to your question is no."

"Okay, Vera."

"Vera?"

"That's your new nickname. Short for veracity. Or Vera Ornery. Take your pick. But it's still Vera."

"Do I have a choice?"

"Yes and no, but I'm leaning toward the no."

"Okay. It's better than my other nickname, a lot better. My other nickname was FB, which was short for Fat Bitch. Julie Murphy got the idea off of Austin Powers when we were in something like fourth grade—she just modified it for me, and the girls used to call me that and laugh. I couldn't do anything about it so I just tried to ignore it, but it got around. I'm surprised that you didn't hear it."

"I didn't, but I wasn't doing an investigation. I like Vera a lot better."

"Me too."

"I'm glad you like it, Vera, because I don't want to have to start calling you FB."

"I really appreciate that, Tommie Boy, Runner Dude. I could think up a few really good names for you." For starters, how about *Why do you care*?

"You mean other than Tommy Boy and Runner Dude? When's that gonna happen? Okay, I'll bet you could, and you might , but I know, being the kind person that you are, you won't actually use them."

"You got me there, Tommie. Oh yeah, I'm so kind, like not at all. Anyway, there's always Runner Dude." Is this turning into an actual conversation? When did we leave the metaconversation? Maybe that's the best way to leave: you don't know you're doing it. And I was doing my best to keep it from happening. I should just shut up and get the hell out of here.

"I know I didn't actually answer your question, Vera, you know, about my life. The best I can say is, sometimes I feel very sad, really sad, and confused and hopeless, and sometimes I feel hopeful, like all the sadness and suffering is leading to *something*. I get that hopeful feeling sometimes when I'm running—even in the middle of a really painful race, even when I know that the race itself doesn't really mean anything and there's no extrinsic reward for running it. Especially since I mostly suck. Just being out there seems hopeful, somehow, so it's almost like being happy, if only for a moment, or even if only in retrospect—like now, when I'm telling you about it. It feels like everything is okay, or, at least that it *will be* okay. That's the hopeful part. Then, there's the thing about being out there with the other guys that makes it feel like I have some connection to the human race—even if they're a bunch of mutants like Ferris and Harlan—especially Harlan."

I actually find myself laughing out loud at that last comment. I think it's the first spontaneous laugh I've felt in at least two years. No, it's got to be longer. Weird. Maybe it's the behemoth chocolate. Harlan and Ferris are both mutants. I've got to agree.

There was a lull in the conversation, and then Tommie continued.

"Did you think that was funny? You're not saying anything. What's the problem, has Big Brother got your tongue?"

"My mind has been abducted by Homeland Security."

"Well, Vera, that *could* be a good thing. But my impression is that your mind has been abducted by aliens from Uranus."

Tommie really starts laughing, and I can't help from laughing. I actually laugh for a good ten seconds. Holy shit, is my mind being abducted by aliens? Why do I have to *fight* everything? Why do I have to be suspicious? "It's got to be an improvement, that's all I can say. Are you here to take me to your planet, your planet Uranus?"

"That's possible, Vera, but first you've got to pass the screening process. Is everything okay...with you? Is happiness possible on your planet, or is it only a mirage instituted to manipulate an otherwise desperate population?"

"If I pass this test, is there another one before I can beam up?"

"Well, there's the ten mile run and the one thousand situps."

"I guess I ain't gonna make it to Uranus any time soon."

"Okay, we'll skip the second part. You've only got to answer that one question: is everything okay on your planet?"

"Ass-tro Tommie, it's not. It's really not." No, no, did I say that? It didn't sound like I was joking either. I can't look at him now. Shit. Don't want to cry. Shit. I'm feeling the pressure behind my eyes. I look down and keep looking down.

Tommy does not seem fazed. "It's okay if it's not. Maybe it will get better. Maybe you need more oxygen on your planet, or more trees or something. Or more Ass-tro men."

"One is enough." Shit, that sounded like an insult. That's why I never try to say anything good about anybody—it always comes out as an insult. I'm such a blubbering bitch. My eyes are feeling puffy. I should have stayed home and read J.D. Salinger or Kurt Vonnegut or *Nausea* over again for about the fifteenth time.

"That's handy, Vera, 'cause I'm the only inhabitant on my planet. You only get one Ass-tro

Tommie man, and believe me, that's *all* you want. Ass-tro man is unruly and unkempt…."

"My mom is sick." Did I just blurt that out? Maybe I didn't really say it at all, I just thought it. God, I feel dizzy. It's so freakin' hot in here. I'll have to look at Tommie to see if he heard. I think he was still talking, so he probably missed it. If not, I'm not saying *another word* for the rest of the day. I promise. I can get out of here in one piece if I keep my yap shut. I've got to get it together. I've got to. Just shut the fuck up.

"What was that, Monica?"

He's looking right at me. His blue eyes are right there in my space. I'm gonna have to say something. "My mom is sick. She…She…She's got breast cancer and it's bad." I'm not gonna be able to stop myself. God, my eyes hurt. It is hot as hell in here.

"Boy, I didn't know…I didn't…Uh, I'm sorry to hear…."

There was a long silence. I stared at my cup of hot chocolate and tried to hold back the tears.

"Monica, it's okay if you cry. It's…It's a good thing. You… you really care about your mom."

Another long silence, except for me whimpering and blubbering.

"If you want to get out of here, we can just go."

Do I ever want to get out of here. Do I ever.

"You don't have to finish your drink or anything if you don't want to. We can just leave the mugs here."

I can't speak. I'll sound like a whining baby. God. I want to hide but there's nowhere to hide. God, is it cold in here?

"Here, just leave your mug, and let's just walk over to the door, and we can walk the back way to your house."

"Okay." I'm sobbing and I sound pathetic, but he's being really nice about it. I make it to the door, but I feel kind of sick to my stomach. Tommie is holding onto my arm as he pushes the door open with his other arm. I hate everything. I feel weak. I feel sick in my stomach.

"Tommie, I can't...sorry." That's about the weakest, most pathetic sentence I've ever heard coming out of my mouth. What a goddamn shitty day, what a goddamn shitty day. Uranus or anywhere but here. I stumble down the few steps to the sidewalk, clutching Tommie's arm. I'm in a stupor during the five-block walk back home. I know Tommie's walking with me, but I can't think straight. I feel angry as well as sad. I feel like I'm groping around in a fog. It takes me most of the way home before I can form a coherent sentence, or before I can hear much at all. There's this ringing in my ears, and I feel so dizzy and lightheaded. I'm getting ready to vomit, but nothing comes up. Nothing keeps coming up.

"Monica, I'm really sorry to hear about your mother...I didn't know about it...Thanks for telling me. It must be very hard for you. I don't really know what you're going through."

"You... had no way of knowing. My dad doesn't want anyone to know outside of the immediate family, but it's been... almost two years." My throat feels tight. I'm in trouble now.

"Two years is a long time to keep a secret like that. Sometimes it can be good to keep secrets, but a lot of times it's not a good thing and it really takes a toll on you." That is so true. For almost two years I've been living in dread about what would happen to my mom and living in dread that someone would find out that she was sick. *Why does it have to be a secret?* Why? I realize that I'm shaking. We're walking so slowly that it's going to take an eternity to get back to my house.

"Tommie, am I...shaking?"

"Yes, Vera, you're trembling a little." I get this feeling that he's being overly kind.

"How long have I been shaking like this?"

"Oh, for a little while. It's okay, you're

upset. You've got a lot on your mind." How long has it been since someone actually listened to me and was kind? How long? I don't think I can remember back that far. Or maybe I'm the one that's not listening.

"Was I shaking back at the café?"

"Aahh, yeah, but only the last few minutes." I think I was right about Tommie. God I hope so. I hope he doesn't tell anybody. We're at the end of my driveway and all I can think about is running into the house, going straight to my room, slamming the door, and hiding. But I have to ask Tommie one thing first.

"Tommie, will you please not tell anyone about my mother? And please don't say anything about the café?" I sound like I'm groveling.

"Hey, there's only Ass-tro man on my planet, and he ain't givin' up no secrets." He's trying to be upbeat, but now I'm really feeling weak and sick to my stomach. I've got to get in the house. "But you can visit my planet and talk about it whenever you like."

"Thanks, Tommie." I'm barely audible. "I have to go now."

"Sure. We can talk again later. I'm glad you told me." I feel like I'm going to pass out. I walk as fast as I safely can, which is more like a moon walk stagger, get inside the door, make it to my room, slam the door, and jump face down on the bed. When I wake up, it's the next morning.

*   *   *   *   *

Tommie stood at the end of the Le Blanc driveway, but it felt like the end of the world. He checked his Timex Ironman. It was 9:27:41 p.m. He had a lot on his mind. He walked the six blocks back to his place and entered through the back door as always. His mom and dad were watching TV. Well, not exactly. The TV was on some forensic show. Somebody had bumped off somebody they pretended to love, and then tried to conceal the evidence. When the body was found at the bottom of a local lake, tied to some large rocks, the lover denied any involvement. God, was that an old plot. If only it were fiction. Especially the pretending to love part. They should just make it a law that nobody can say they love anybody else, thought Tommie, that way, the homicide rate will be reduced by something like seventy-eight percent right there. The volume was loud, too loud, but not too loud to sleep through if you just worked a seventy-hour week. Tommie turned off the set manually. He didn't even bother to look for the remote. He knew it was probably somewhere under Dad, or under the recliner, or some other undisclosed location. Mom was peering through her reading half-glasses at the local paper. On closer inspection, her eyes were closed, and it looked like they had been for some time. Dad was snoring in the faux lazy-boy, all the way back. It was a typical night.

Tommie went up to his room and got out his running clothes. He had too much on his mind to go to sleep. What better way to deal with it than an easy night run? Ten minutes later he was gliding down West Charlotte Street. Tommie observed each house as he passed noiselessly through the cloudless night and into his future. He was beginning to break a sweat and his easy, rhythmic respiration felt in synch with whatever was out there. He was on the outside of the American dream, looking in. A pervasive sense of palpable absence led him down each quiet street. Was he chasing the wistfulness of youth, or fleeing the cynicism of adulthood? Bluish light illuminated window after window. Dreams without end lurked inside. The light of television after television and computer after computer lit up home after home as he took step after step down street after street into future after future without end without end.

15

PHILOSOPHERS AND OTHER MISCREANTS

Ferris lets out a gigantic yawn, a yawn so enormous that it looks like he might lose his balance and fall right the hell out of his chair. He saves it at the last second, and then lets out the coda, another yawn with a small belch on the end. If the first was an 8.2 on the Richter scale, the last was a 6.2. Both nasty bad. Winter was out in the hall, boondoggling and harassing hapless students with his Bette Davis eyes and their spooky lasers that could burn right through you. Today, that is a good thing, or Ferris would have had after school suspension for sure. True, there isn't any cross-country meet, but sometimes wayward students get more than a day in the after school slammer, so you never know what's going to happen when you let out a couple of heavy Richter scale yawns.

They say yawning is contagious, and I agree. I've seen it many times at this joint. But I'd also like to submit that stupidity is contagious, and ignorance too. Pardon me, I'm feeling a nasty yawn coming on. It's up there on the Richter scale. After first and second period, anything's possible. At this point, most of us should get a medal for just being conscious. Personally, I'd prefer two study halls any day to my first and second period classes. What the?—it's Harlan letting out a power yawn. I told you those things were contagious. I know Monica is behind me. I just glanced back there but she wasn't looking in my direction. We haven't said much to each other since last Saturday, but she sent me a few texts. I think she's avoiding me, but I'm not positive. I'd probably avoid me too if I could.

Winter walks in. He doesn't just walk in, he walks in like it's something special. I mean, he *walks in*. Maybe when you're *that* old, it is something special, 'cause nobody's *wheeling* you in: you're actually moving your low bone density, osteoarthritic legs under your own steam. How old is he? I have no idea, but anybody that looks over triple our age might as well be living in the Old Testament. He's got the gray vest, brown slacks with cuffs, pale blue shirt with sleeves rolled up like he's gonna actually do some work or something, and 19th century leather shoes, probably from when he attended the one room school house in 1887 over in Craley in York County on the Susquehanna River. I avoid the laser eyes 'cause I don't want to do any full pipe singing. I'm barely living down the infamy from last week. I can still hardly believe I survived it.

"Welcome philosophers and other miscreants!" Winter belts out like he's on Broadway.

"What's a mist-cre-ant?" Zeferino is whispering in my right ear and tapping me on the shoulder at the same time. He sounds like *he's* got to be a mistcreant.

"I don't know, dude. Something bad. Now shut up," I whisper, without turning my head.

Suddenly Winter's eyes affix on Zeferino. "Mr. Zeferino, please stand," Winter practically yells. Holy crap, that loser Zeferino. He should have just kept it closed, but no, inquiring minds want to know. I'm already breaking out in a sweat, and we're like ninety seconds into class. It takes Kenny something like a near eternity to actually get his butt off the seat. If you think it's bad now, wait until he has low bone density and osteoarthritis.

"Did you have a question, or something to share with the class, Mr. Zeferino?" Winter toys with the hapless Z man. Well, yeah, but it was all his fault. Oh God, it's the Bette Davis eyes. The front of the class is hypnotized.

"Why, yes sir. What's a mist-cre-ant, sir?" What a dork. Don't ask questions and you'll get along just fine. Didn't he learn anything at all in all these years of public education?

"A *mis*creant! Good word. Where'd you get it?" If I can stay out of trouble for forty-three more minutes, I won't have to sing…today. That's all I'm thinking.

"Sir, you used the term a moment ago, sir, if I'm not mist-tak-en." Dorkdorkdorkdorkdork.

"No, Mr. Zeferino, you are not a *mist-*

taken *mist*-creant. A *mis*-creant is a depraved, heretical, villainous infidel. Thanks for asking."

"So…ah yeah…that sounds like a bad thing." Winterfield has awakened from his dogmatic slumber.

"You're quick on the draw, Winterfield." Sarcasm or not? Who's to know?

"Thank you, Dr. Winter." Winterfield is actually sitting up straight in his seat, a once-in-a-lifetime event. Usually, the back of his neck is resting on the top of his seat back and he's bordering on comatose. And that's on a good day. Maybe he's just saving it for the meet, conserving energy by hibernating in class. But not today.

"Absolutely, Winterfield." Winter and Winterfield, together again, live at the Shuck 'n Jive Theatre in Branson, Missouri. Damn, I can't seem to focus on much of anything. Winter walks back up to the front and gets a serious look on his face. I'm thinking Abraham Lincoln and Robert Duvall and Clint Eastwood all at the same time. I hear Zeferino's faint doplic laugh coming from behind. Dumb-ass. "Now, to the topic for today. We are going to discuss *the most important philosophical issue ever*: the nature of the human being. If you get this wrong, you end up being wrong about *everything* else, and I mean *everything* else. Having a correct read on the human being is the starting point for all correct philosophizing, so we've got to tread carefully here. I am going to build a case for my position on this issue, so be careful to note not only what I am saying, but the very process I am employing to build a case for something. Not to be pompous, but it will be an *example* regarding how to go about the process of philosophizing." Oh no, not pompous at all.

I keep waiting for the punch line. Then I realize that Winter's demeanor really *has* changed; he is serious—in a good way. I obliquely observe the Bette Davis eyes, for no one can cast his eyes upon the face of the almighty—and live.

"I'd like to start with an example to shed some light on the nature of the human being. Later, this illustration will shed some light on the current financial crisis and its real causes. None of you has to pay income taxes—yet—but be assured, soon enough you will be forking over plenty to the wonderful Internal Revenue Service. Some of you pay Social Security and Medicare/Medicaid right now. Jason Lake, you're paying it. Isn't that right?"

"Ah, yeah, I guess so. My check is like almost zero after my twenty hours a week. After they take all that crap out, I'm lucky if I get 115 bucks. It sucks."

"Now tell us how you *really* feel, Mr. Lake." Lake sits up straight in his seat, something

I haven't seen since about the fourth grade. First it's Winterfield, now Lake. What the hell's going on here?

"I feel like I'm getting ripped off. If they want to take all that, they should pay me more, that's all I've got to say." His voice is loud. "At this rate, I've got to work two or three months to pay for one college course at the state university, so you know I can never pay my way through—ever. I'd be something like forty years old until I paid it off." His voice is getting even louder. "And that's if I actually *get* a real job." He pauses and looks down. He seems to have caught himself and backs off on the volume. He's looking at the backs of his hands, stretched out on his desktop. "It didn't used to be like that. My parents both worked their way through the state college, and they didn't take out loans. I was planning on doing the same thing, but it doesn't look good."

Lake actually sounds mighty pissed off and sad all at the same time, and he's one of the lucky bastards *with* an actual job. Or, at least what passes for one. So that's what I've got to look forward to. Oh yeah. I can't wait.

"I saw you at Taco Belch, so I know you're paying into Social Security and Medicare/Medicaid—and if you earn enough, you'll be paying income tax, even if you don't want to. Even if they dismantle all those social programs before *you* get a dime, you're paying into them now, or you can't work. Unless you get paid in cash under the table, in which case you could be subject to arrest, prosecution, a little time in the slammer and all that jazz. So, you're paying them. Remember, we needed to bail out those multinational, multibillion dollar financial institutions like Bank of Fleece-America, All Infidels Group, CitiFustercluck and Oldmensch Suchs because they were *too big to fail*— according to Ben Bernanke, Chairman of the Federal Reserve, and Henry Paulson before him. Bernanke said he *needed to hold his nose* and orchestrate the bailouts; I have to hold my nose whenever someone utters the name 'Bernanke'. *You're* not too big to fail. The question is: *are you too small to succeed?*" I'm feeling too small to participate. Are there any habitable planets where it's a lot easier to just live and get along? Why the heck is everything so freakin' complicated on planet earth? It must be the humans.

What the...? Ferris is actually raising his hand. Winter stares in his direction.

"It's Ben *Ber-spank-me*, sir." He just sits there. Slowly, there is not-so-suppressed laughter.

"Nice one, Ferris. Nice one. Berspankme. Perfect. That's exactly what he's doing.

Quantitative easing, my ass. QE1, QE2.

Berspankme. Berspankyou. Nice." Winter looks pleased.

I look around. People are actually paying attention. Weird. I feel too small to succeed. I thought we were talking about capitalism. Too big to fail doesn't even make any sense to me. Isn't it supposed to be all about the free market, with open competition and that stuff? So, why give money to the loser so he stays in the game and doesn't lose? He's already *proven* that he can't make it on the open market, that he's a loser. What more do you need to know? So why give him more money—that would be *our money*—so that he can go right back to losing? Does that make any sense? I guess, if you're against a free market economy. My bullshit detector is going off. Weird. I see a bird fly by the windows. It lands about fifty feet up in a maple tree. A good spot to observe our classroom. Definitely above all the temporal machinations going on down here, you know, all the stuff we've invented to make life so much harder for ourselves. Yeah, we had to learn that word—machinations—in Winter's class. A good one too. Really useful. Now, it seems to apply to everything. Okay, I take that back. It seems to apply to everything having to do with *humans*. Anyway, Winter makes us actually learn the words we don't know in our readings. How the hell else are we going to learn them?

Osmosis? Telepathy? Genetic engineering? Free market ingenuity? And there's that bird, sitting right up there in that maple tree looking down. I wish I knew what kind of bird that was, but I basically have no clue. Flying like that must be cool. Here I am spacing it again. My attention is drawn back to Winter's voice, or maybe I just got to the end of my daydream. Maybe Winter can't think unless he's moving because he's all over the place, shuffling around like nobody's business. He fades back in.

"...Okay...Let's imagine that paying income taxes is voluntary. You'd be able to calculate what you owe, but sending the money was on the honor system, and there'd be no penalty for nonpayment. How many of you would pay?" I was wondering if he was way off the topic or not. It didn't take long to go around the room. There were about two people who said they would pay, and they probably didn't even understand the question. Does anybody really know what they would do unless they were actually in that situation? Can you really know what you'd do in advance? Yeah, right. I doubt it. In your fantasy, you'd play the Good Samaritan, and then when it got right down to it, you'd keep the money. Oh, yeah, there'd be a few Mother Teresas out there, but otherwise, people would keep the dough and rationalize that they could put it to so much better use than the freakin' government. That's why paying taxes isn't voluntary. If people would actually send in the money *voluntarily*, you could dump the whole stupid IRS. Yeah, and that's gonna happen. Looks like I spaced it again. Winter's somewhere behind me, paripateting around the back of the classroom.

"...It looks to me like over ninety percent of you wouldn't pay your taxes if they were voluntary. Now the question is: why not?" Wasn't it obvious? Not to Winter. Nothing seems obvious to him. Stupid philosopher. Nothing is ever obvious to a philosopher. No wonder all they do is think.

"You might think, theoretically, that each person should pay his or her fair share, but *you* don't believe that the system assesses you your fair share, so *you're* not inclined to pay. But you're also saying that you believe that people *ought* to pay their taxes. You just don't pay yours because you don't think *you* ought to have to pay. Is this consistent or inconsistent?" Everybody was quiet as hell, so Winter kept going. "Or, you might argue that government in general is the problem, that government is a bad thing—beyond very basic services, and so for that reason you don't want to pay *your* taxes. You might call this a Libertarian policy. In this case, if there's a pothole in your road, fix it yourself. Don't rely on the damn government. They're just out to take your money. Well, that's what people of the latter persuasion often maintain." Winter's back up front, walking in circles. The guy must get in a two-mile walk during every philosophy class. That's more exercise than we ever got in gym class. Maybe we should walk with him. It would be an example of herd philosophizing. Maybe the only example, since a reflective herd sounds like an oxymoron to me. Well, even if we're *not* reflecting while we're taking our two mile walk around the room, at least we'd be getting some exercise, and not sitting in the rock-hard chair/desk combos. That's gotta be a good thing, right?

"Now, it turns out that the overwhelming majority, in fact, go with the first reason when they say they don't want to pay their taxes. They maintain that people *ought* to pay their taxes, that it would be a good thing if everyone were to pay them, but they would not end up paying *theirs*. *They* would be, somehow, an *exception*. So, over ninety percent of people would think it was a good thing to pay one's taxes, and that it would be wrong or morally wrong not to pay one's taxes, but *these same people would find a rationale for not paying their own taxes*. Morality, then, is for *other people*, unless, of course, your self-interest coincides with the moral thing to do, in which case, you would act in a self-interested way and still be doing the moral thing, but not for moral reasons." Winter starts walking around to the back of the room. What the heck is he saying? Sounds like he's saying people are basically SOBs. But the SOBs think they are Good Samaritans. That's got to be the worst-case scenario. Nice.

"My argument is that this process and type of reasoning is universal and pervasive, and that it is our basic approach in real world decision-making when dealing with others—with very few exceptions. We state unequivocally what we think the right course of action would be, and then we find a way to employ all the powers of our intellect—combined with self-deception and boundless hubris—to excuse ourselves from having to follow the very course of action that we, only moments before, knew to be the right course of action. Why even bother to get the facts and think for yourself, if, in the end, you are simply going to do what seems to be in your own self-interest anyway and the hell with anybody else? Because that's what we're saying here: regardless of economic or social class, educational background or any other identifiable variable, the vast majority of people will not do what *they themselves* deem to be the right thing unless *forced* to do it. They will rationalize that somehow they are an exception to the very rule that they state is valid." Winter wasn't finished yet. Not nearly. You could see it in his eyes. He was just warming up.

"Therefore, as a consequence, we've got thousands of employees at the IRS, and we grant the organization nearly unlimited power to track you down and put you in jail if you don't pay your taxes—and even with that power, millions of people are still managing to rip off everybody else. We know from historical example that without the threat of severe punishment for nonpayment of taxes the government would be defunded in days, and the government/nation/state as we know it would become merely a matter of historical record. What does this tell you about the nature of the human being?" Damn. I need some powdered orange Gatorade. Or, better yet, some Chicken Mountain iced tea. Maybe about two gallons.

"What does hoo-brus mean? Tosha Monette asks. Good question. I have no freakin' idea myself. It sounds like a dreaded social disease.

"Miss...LeBlanc!" I keep my head low but swivel my neck back and to the left. Monica has her hand up. Wow.

"Hubris is when humans start thinking

they're God, or even better than God. It's a Greek concept. For the Greeks, when people started getting a little hubris, it meant it was time for a god or two to come down and kick their asses." Vera's eyes were all puffy and it didn't look like she had slept in a week, but damn was I proud of her. Hubris or no hubris. She did have on that hard to miss rumpled mustard sweater she was wearing at the café.

"Absolutely, Miss LeBlanc! Outstanding." Winter looked very pleased. "Especially the ass kicking part. Thank you. Thank you very much. You do not have to pay your taxes until 2020, and by then, it probably won't even matter." Bette Davis was back in town. Watch the eyes, watch the eyes.

"Is that...comforting?" Monica asked. She needs to run a good 5K cross-country race. It'll put world geo-politics and human nature in perspective, as only heinous pain can do.

"Only if you can change...human nature, or the nature of the human being." For some reason, Winter was sending a chill down my spine: it was like an arctic blast. My brain was full. But I was starting to like that mustard sweater.

Winter was not about to stop making his point. He was going to think it through until the end, or until the bell, whichever came first.

"Let's go back to our conclusion based on the results derived from the voluntary tax payment example: the vast majority of people will *not* do what *they themselves* deem to be the right thing unless *forced* to do it. They will rationalize that somehow they are an exception to the very rule that they state is valid. Human nature clearly tends toward the irrational when self-interest or perceived self-interest is at stake.

"Now imagine that investment brokers and others working in the financial markets, futures, complex derivatives and all the rest of that bogus swill, can buy off the government so that the government deregulates old markets and investment vehicles and fails to regulate new markets and investment vehicles. And if the regulations cannot be effectively repealed by Congress, as in the case of FDR's Glass-Steagall Act, which *did* regulate markets until it was gutted by Phil Gramm and Bill Clinton and a few other thugs at the very end of the 20th century—then the financial sector simply buys off the regulators in the regulatory institutions, so that existing regulations have absolutely no teeth.

"Next, the financial sector needs to control or eliminate the ratings agencies like Muddy's— they have to buy them off or bring them inside the fold—so that the ratings will stay where they need to be and unwary investors will still mistake shit for gold, which they did to the tune of $640 trillion in the OTD market—Over-The-Counter-Derivatives—at the time of the collapse in the fall of 2008. I know, it sounds like over-the-counter cough medicine, only this stuff doesn't make you better, it makes you sick as hell. It's economic poison, a time bomb, a hot potato, and the financial sector benefits when you're caught holding the potato. Everything is orchestrated so that you—we—are caught holding the potato." I could use a few potatoes right about now. Potato chips. Yeah, salt and vinegar potato chips. Or maybe a couple of tater tots. My mouth is watering as my stomach growls. I try hard to regain my focus.

Winter affected a nasally, high-pitched voice: "...We were so blindsided by the economic meltdown. We *didn't know* it could happen." A Wall Street swindler, no doubt. Then he went back to his usual tone: "All that's a load of shit they feed you calculated to sucker you back in—after you've been stuck with the hot potato that blew up in your face, or, you might say, the home that just dropped fifty percent in value since you bought it four years ago. If *they* get caught holding the hot potato, well then *you* bail *them* out, because *they* are so necessary to *your* survival. That's *their* story. The real truth is that *you and your gullibility* are necessary for their survival. If they were gone, you'd be much better off, since they're skimming the lion's share and making you thank them for it.

"Finally, the *persona ficta*—the corporate entity— juridical persons—must find a way to bribe the accounting agencies—like Enron did with Arthur Anderson—so that any financial improprieties or illegal activities will not be uncovered—at least not before the criminals get their loot and are safely in some undisclosed location on foreign soil from which there is no extradition treaty with the U.S.A. The result: the wild west, or as English philosopher Thomas Hobbes would say, the *state of nature*, where life is 'solitary, poor, nasty, brutish and short.' Or, using our example: the people with the vast majority of the money can decide for themselves if they want to pay their taxes. This is the state of nature, or pre-civilization, if you will.

"Now, let's go back to our pre-established basic principle, a principle derived from the observation of thousands of years of human history, a universal principle rooted in the nature of the human being: the vast majority of people *will not do* what *they themselves* deem to be the right thing unless *forced* to do it. They will rationalize that somehow they are an exception to the very rule that they state is valid. If you want more evidence of this basic principle of human nature, go back and read the earliest *tour de force* in the field of history based on inductive data collection: Thucydides' *History of the Peloponnesian War*. The Greek city-states, in all their glory and hubris, are categorical evidence for our basic principle of human nature. This principle of human nature is derived from the observation of thousands of years of human history, and cuts across cultural, geopolitical, racial, and ethnic lines. It is a universal principle rooted in the nature of the human being, wherever he or she may be found." Salt and vinegar? Mesquite Barbeque? Tots? I need some freakin' tots. The growling seems to be getting louder. Hot or cold, I'll take some taters right about now.

"Now, back to us. What do we know about unregulated markets? Those operating in such markets are not forced to do the right thing, whatever that may be. This is a matter of the definition of a truly free market, hence, a self-evident truth. And based upon our pre-established principle, these people will not in fact act for the good of the society, but will act out of self-interest. They will sell shit for gold, even when they are being paid to advise the person to whom they sold the shit—in fact, *especially* to the person to whom they sold the shit—since that's the most proximate and therefore available person *and* the person with whom they have a fiduciary relationship ripe for exploitation. That would be the definition of fiduciary obligation—to act in the best financial interest *of your client*. No significant sign of that in the current market. It's a quaint notion from a bygone era, or a mythological era. It's your call on that one. Someone like Bernard Madoff could not exist in a climate where there were even skeletal regulations, with a minimal level of verified disclosure. There wasn't a minimal level of regulation and so we got Bernie Madoff and thousands of others who bilked the hell out of every mom and pop investor and guy with a few bucks in his 401K. This behavior is the real threat to our society, the real terror to our society." This is the real terror? The real terror is when your feel like you're gonna barf all over the place at the league cross-country meet right in front of about 225 runners on twenty-eight teams and a bunch of coaches and a few actual spectators and you can't run fast enough to make it off the starting line and down the stadium steps and into the parking lot before you blow your guts so you just look down while you're standing on the starting line with the 225 guys and barf all over your fancy ass Pine Manor singlet and shorts. Seconds later, the starting gun goes off and you lurch forward with vomit sliming down your face and legs and uniform. And then you find a full body color photo of yourself in the next day's Sunday edition sports section of the local paper, plastered with barf. Oh yeah, now that's livin'. It's the stuff of legends. It happened to Harlan last year. Awesome, but not for him. And here I am back in la-la land. I glance stealthily at my watch. 28 minutes down, 23 to go. And I even like this class. Boy do I suck. Am I just what Winter is talking about? An aspiring lazy-ass freeloader who thinks he's an exception to the rules? Winter fades back in.

"...If the one percent of the population that has fifty-plus percent of the capital and investments is on the honor system to disclose its wealth, activities, the true nature of its product, and the veracity of the infomercials it peddles to the sycophantic media, what will it do? Think about what's best *for you*? What's best for our society? Are these guys patriotic? Hell, no! If they cause an implosion and our society collapses completely, they'll be at their second house in Paris, or their third house in Rio, or their fourth house in the Costa Rica, or their bunker in Somalia, or their secret compound in Qatar before you even wake up the next morning.

"They'll be out of the country before you can even get to the post office to renew your passport, or apply for a passport, or whatever it is you think you're going to do to get out of the cesspool the one percent have created for everybody else. The only problem with your plan is that the post office won't be open yet, and it probably won't be opening at all today, or tomorrow, or the next day. Vandals will break in, and later some street people might sleep in there, but as for a United States Post Office, well, that's just an historical curiosity. It will be gone forever. We don't need World War III for all of this to happen, people. We don't need armed conflict on U.S. soil for this to happen. Wake up! Look at the national debt and then explain last month's federal tax cuts to this same one percent of the population, the same one percent that lobbied for and got the deregulation that allows them to act solely in their self-interest, taking billions of dollars and providing no real product or service, even if *you* have to work yourself into an early grave at $8.25 an hour just to keep a roof over your head—if your job hasn't been sent overseas by these very same people. They're robbing you coming and going.

"If we—I mean everyone in this room—don't make some enormous systemic changes, there will be no future—unless by future you mean universal slave economy. And it is your future we are talking about. *Your* future. Right now, you are all victims of the largest propaganda campaign the world has ever known, fueled by twenty-four hour news cycles run and fed by multinational media conglomerates in bed with the military-industrial-medical complex, a complex that funds and creates the only political candidates for whom you will ever be able to vote, and these votes will inevitably and necessarily betray your interests, but they will not betray the indelibly antithetical interests of that one percent."

Winter paused, stopped walking, and started staring around the room. Holy shit, not me. Please, not me. I don't want to have to do any more involuntary Madame Xero *Big Man* a cappella karaoke, even if it is a pretty cool tune. I mean, Madame Xero is great, yeah, as long as I don't have to do any more singing in class. Luckily, a voice splits the silence. It's Skip Garnet, harrier god. *Yes.*

"Dr. Winter. I've got a question."

"Easy or hard?"

"Easy to ask, hard to answer, I guess." Those farm boys have got a way with words.

"Are you saying that those rich people you're talking about are more evil than us regular folk? Is that what you're saying? That they got there because they're more evil, or something like that?"

"Mr. Garnet, great question. You're thinking it through! Some people have *possibly* maintained that position, and I think there is evidence for this point of view. For example, check out Dr. Martha Stout, a psychiatrist, author of the book *The Sociopath Next Door*—which I highly recommend, by the way— for what *that's* worth. Maybe we'll read it next spring for this class and then we could discuss the implications of her findings on public policy and economic inequality. So—you've got that to look forward to. Could this class get *any* better? Sociopathy may well be an important contributory factor when we're talking about contemporary business and political leaders. But that thesis is stronger than what I am arguing—I'm not going that far, not because I don't think it's true—I do—but because I don't think we need to go that far, it wouldn't produce any tangible benefit, and it may lead us on a witch hunt. And God knows there've been far too many of *those* in the history of humankind—in fact, that might be a thoroughly adequate thumbnail summation of the history of humankind: we've moved from one witch hunt to another. As long as you're looking for the next witch, you never have to look at yourself. And, if you remember, we started this class with a question about what *you* would do, whether *you* would voluntarily pay your taxes if you weren't forced to do it—if you knew you could get away with not paying them, if the whole income tax thing was a voluntary program. And remember, almost all of you said you wouldn't pay."

"So, you're not saying that the rich are worse than we are? They're not more evil?" asked John Raush, the Bible dude. He was still conscious, and he wasn't quoting scripture. Two thumbs up.

"Exactly, Mr. Raush. Those rich bloodsuckers aren't any more evil than you or I. If they were more evil than I am, they'd have horns!" Harlan let out a loud stupid laugh, almost a guffaw. Winter stopped, pinned Harlan with his laser beams, and then continued. "They just have an opportunity that we currently do not have— however they got it—an opportunity to exercise greed and malfeasance to the nth degree, and, as we have seen throughout world history, this power rarely goes unexercised; and once exercised, it is seldom relinquished."

"I'll have to agree with you there. For all have sinned and come short of the glory of God. Romans chapter three and verse twenty three." Okay, now he's quoting scripture, but it seems to agree with what Winter is saying. I wasn't even too sure what the hell Raush was doing in the class, but he seemed to like what Winter was saying. I liked it too. I never did think those people at Credit Card City were my friends. They weren't friends with my parents either. Winter was walking all around the room—

behind us, on both sides of the room, the regular peripatetic. I thought he meant dietetic or something like that, but he always said peripatetic, so I had to look that one up too. I was getting nervous. My vocal chords were on my mind. It's hard to get used to some big guy walking behind you and then just standing there. Especially if he's haranguing you about economic justice or something. But somehow, it tends to keep you awake. But I *still* manage to space it pretty often. Pathetic. Winter's peripateting back where I can see him. And I almost fall out of my chair when he brings up his habit of peripateting. Can this guy read my mind?

"I've been called the pathetic peripatetic, always tilting at windmills. True insanity is to accept the world as it is, and not as it should be! So said the *Man of La Mancha*, Don Quixote! Listen philosophers, don't let the cynics steal your hope. We lose our humanity when we lose our hope, our dreams are gone, our true passion submerged, our real feelings obliterated. There is nothing left but to create an artificial universe based upon our own self-deception, a place where we can hide from our true selves and the calling of a very real world in need. False stimulation is the order of the day in such an artificial universe, a universe devoid of hope, which means a universe devoid of love. Don't let anyone rob you of what is central to your humanity—your hope."

"Did you say you're a paraplegic?" inquires Harlan. He's gonna rip Harlan a new one. That bastard would poke a hornet's nest. Why doesn't Harlan just keep a lid on it? Such an anus.

"Peripatetic, not paraplegic. It's a world of difference, Harlan. A world of difference. What is a peripatetic, Mr. Harlan? You *should* have looked it up. You've heard it in here before, which means you'd better know it, right?" Suddenly, the boot was all the way up on Harlan's kindergarten desk. Pretty flexible for an old crazy guy. Harlan was staring at Winter's boot with a deranged look of knowing he was going too far. And he wasn't finished yet.

"Is that real leather, or fake leather?" asks Harlan, angling for 1000 years of after school suspension.

"Why do you care, Mr. Harlan? Are you a PETA spy? It's going to feel just the same either way, if you catch my drift."

"You're advocating violence, Dr. Winter?"

Winter knew Harlan's dad was an English Professor over at the University, so he gave Harlan a particularly hard time, which means something, since he often came off as a real asshole under normal circumstances.

"I would never advocate violence, per se, Mr. Harlan, but under certain circumstances, you––or should I say I—may have no alternative."

"Aahh, you mean like when the U.S. invaded Iraq?" Harlan has a death wish. This can only end badly. I glanced at my watch, furtively. Maybe he will be saved by the bell, but I doubt it. We've still got a good sixteen or seventeen minutes left in this shakedown.

"That's precisely what I *don't* mean, Mr. Harlan, which must mean, if I am to understand you correctly, that you understand what I *do* mean."

"Exactly, Dr. Winter. I understand completely. By the way, peripatetic means wandering, walking, or traveling."

"You miscreant. Thanks for holding out. You'll make a great philosopher."

"Thanks, but I plan on being the new Prefontaine. The world is way overdue." Harlan had extricated himself with reckless abandon, and it worked. But who the hell is going to know who Prefontaine is, except maybe a cross-country runner, the scum of all scum?

"In that case, you've only got seven or eight years to live. Better get running. And a lot faster, too." Touché, Winter dude. He *even knows* who Prefontaine is. Now, that *is* shocking. Pretty cool for an obvious non-runner.

I mean, who else cares? Even I'm gonna kick Harlan's butt. New Prefontaine, my ass. How about new Britney Spears cross dresser?

Things really started to get interesting when Ferris piped up: "The only thing about Harlan that reminds me of Prefontaine is the way he's always throwing up during the workout." Harlan *has* thrown up a lot—and not just at the league meet. I think Harlan actually threw up one time—on Ferris. There was quite a bit of laughter after Ferris insulted Harlan. Even John Raush laughed. So did Harlan, but he kind of looked like he might throw up. Things are getting good. Amazingly, Winter started peripateting around. Once again, shocking, but in a pedestrian sort of way. He was ready for the final round.

"Ladies and Gentlemen, thank you for your consciousness, and for not throwing up. Before you all do throw up and at the risk of boring you into oblivion, I'd like to recapitulate, which means I'm going to say the same thing over again, so you never forget it, even if you try to forget it: the vast majority of people will not do what *they themselves* deem to be the right thing unless *forced* to do it. They will rationalize that somehow they are an exception to the very rule that *they* state is valid. This is our general working axiom based upon an analysis of historical human behavior—and we've gone back hundreds of years even before the birth of Jesus.

"When we say that we believe something would be *good for everybody to do*, we mean that it would be good if *everybody except us* were to do that thing—but *not* us, because we are somehow an exception to our own stated wisdom. What we are saying, in the end, is that the best possible scenario would be *if everyone else were to do the right thing, but not us*—and if everyone else thought, mistakenly, that we *were* doing the right thing. We don't want to be found out: that would blow our advantage. Is this principle clear to everyone? Any confusion? That's right, if you say yes, I'll rattle on for another ten minutes until you want to commit suicide by falling on your #2 Ticonderoga pencil." In my mind's eye, I saw twenty-seven people falling forward onto their desks, twenty-seven people falling forward on their #2 Ticonderoga pencils. Only Ferris has the strength to speak after all had fallen on their pencils. Gasping, obviously in pain, Ferris wheezes at Winter: "Why, why did you make us fall on our #2 Ticonderoga pencils? Why? Couldn't you have laid off on the economic mumbo jumbo, couldn't you?... Why... Why... Why...?" Ferris slumps over onto his desk and then slowly slides off of his kindergarten desk/chair combo, right onto the square tile floor, arms and legs akimbo, blood oozing from his left pectoral. The room is silent, bodies strewn atop desks, bodies on the floor, face down, face up, crumpled and sprawled, motionless. There is blood dripping off of desks, onto the floor, blood pooling on the square tiles. The blood is so dark it looks like that hot wing sauce they've got down at Jack's Place. A broken #2 Ticonderoga pencil can be seen here and there: the eraser end only, as the twenty-seven sharpened ends have penetrated the chests, souls and possibly the alimentary canals of the young men and women who have given their lives *not to know*, the young men and women who have had the courage to check out before they had to check it out, before they had to investigate the bone chilling tales of the Master of Horror, Dr. Rutherford Urias "Kevorkian" Winter. Give me ignorance or give me death!

Winter slowly pans the room with his Bette Davis eyes, then whips out a crumpled pack of filterless Tareytons. He carefully slides one out, and pulls his chrome lighter from his right hip pocket, flips the top open and brings the flame to the Tareyton dangling from his purplish lips. The cigarette lights up like it's been waiting to be burned for years. Winter takes a drag that's so long the cigarette looks like a sparkler melting down into a purple haze. "Damn, now look what ya'll have made me do. Ya'll have made me start smokin' again. Luckily, I never wash this vest. Damn lucky." Winter turns the Bette Davis lasers back on the scene, panning slowly up and down each row of lifeless bodies, extinguished dreams, decimated hopes, unrealized accomplishments. "Maybe I should go back to dirt farming. Naw, there's already too much of that to go around."

I'm jolted out of my reverie with a start. Winter is standing about fourteen inches in front of me. What the...? He *knows* I'm spacing it.

"Tommie Boy, let's do a little thought experiment, okay?" Why me? Can't he think for himself? Winter isn't going to back down: "Why would a lender want to lend money to someone if the lender knew that the person to whom they were lending the money couldn't pay it back? Said differently, why would you give a mortgage to someone if you knew they couldn't make the payments?" I'm trying to swallow the lump in my throat.

"I wouldn't. That would be just plain stupid." There's got to be a trick here somewhere. I sure hope I don't have to sing any more cutting edge karaoke. God do I hope I don't. I'm feeling hot all over, and not in a good way.

"Exactly. These lenders not only made loans, they advertised day and night to get unqualified customers to sign up for them. Why would they do it?" At least Winter's boot isn't on my desk/chair combo.

"There's got to be some incentive somewhere, or they wouldn't do it," suggests Christine Geist, a comment that seems eminently reasonable to me, especially since Winter's attention is diverted—away from me.

"What if the incentive was selling complex investment vehicles like the over-the-counter derivatives mentioned earlier, vehicles that were like sausage made up of all the sliced and diced innards of the soon-to-default sub-prime mortgages, mortgages so sliced and diced that just about no mortal could ever trace and identify them? And the cool thing is: you invent the recipe for the sausage. It's your recipe and nobody else gets to see it: it's what we call a proprietary recipe. Here you've got the economic hot potato. If you sell a million bucks of these sliced and diced perfumed shit mortgages that are on the road, exceeding the speed limit, heading south, you collect before the hot potato blows, you've cashed out, and *somebody else* gets burnt. The derivatives market, being essentially unregulated, allows you to market shit as gold, so you're in the clear. And remember, voluntary compliance is a euphemism for no regulation.

"Do we need to remember our first basic principle? Remember, ladies and gentlemen: The vast majority of people will not do what *they themselves* deem to be the right thing unless *forced* to do it. They will rationalize that somehow they are an exception to the very rule that they state is valid. There's a lot of fancy artifice in dressing this sausage shit up to look like gold, no doubt. Who knows what the hell is in there? It's the 21st century Frankenstein, the *Blade Runner's* replicant gone trans-human. If there's Agent Orange in that exploding potato, who the hell's gonna figure it out before you're way the hell over on the other side of the planet, nursing your ass on some undisclosed Swiss bank account? Where's the downside?"

"Somebody could go to a gun show in, let's say Cleveland, buy a Glock 9mm semiautomatic, buy a ticket on Amtrak, and then pay you a visit on the 39th floor of your investment firm. They could then proceed to eliminate you and all your slimy primordial ilk from the gene pool so that the world has a hope for justice. That may, on some accounts, be construed as a downside. I'd consider it the only possible upside."

That's John Raush? Oh yeah, big gun dude. Second Amendment rights and all that. Maybe bumping off the investment banker could be construed as an act of self-defense? I'm just protecting my family from the white-collar sociopathic scum that passes for professionalism and expertise in the financial services industry? Absolutely. Things are really getting weird in here.

"Okay, ladies and gentlemen. Let's break it down a little bit. Let's say somebody offers you a thousand dollars for each person you sign up for a special product, but the person offering you the thousand dollars per signature doesn't tell you anything about the product, maintaining that 'All you've got to do is get someone to sign the form, and fill in all the parts that contain an asterisk in the left margin. If they don't want to fill out the rest, that's cool. You don't have to ask them anything, and it's not your job to verify that what they say is true. We'll handle that. Think you can do that? It's easy. All you've got to do is get them to fill out this simple form, that's all there is to it.'"

"How many people would ask questions? Would you still ask questions if your paycheck went from $115.00 per week at Taco Belch to $5,000.00 per week at Shady Financial LLC, and you didn't even have to break a sweat? You wouldn't make most of the money, like the actual sausage makers would, you'd just be the front man to supply some of the raw material to be subsequently sliced and diced by the con chefs. But still, your small slice of the pie results in a

43.47-fold increase in your weekly pay. A year of that, and you could pay *all* of your college tuition––all four years, no problem. Pretty hard to turn down, wouldn't you say? And all you're doing is getting people to sign up for a product that they *can't wait* to get. How could that be a bad thing?"

"I'd do it. If you're dumb enough to take out the loan, that's your damn problem. I'm just offering you something that *you say* you want. And the $5000 bucks a week ain't hurting none either," says Waylon Waites. He seems to be saying what a lot of people are probably thinking right about now. It's hard to dig yourself out of a fifty-foot hole with a two-pint shovel. Working any regular job is certainly a two-pint shovel. Yeah, I've got that part.

"So, you're not hurting anybody directly. You're just setting them up to have the hot potato blow up on 'em later—hopefully far enough down the road so that *you're* not traceable. So, you don't give a rat's ass about them, as long as you get your money. Is that what you're saying, Mr. Waites?" Winter is still peripateting. Now he's somewhere back behind Monica LeBlanc. Man is it nerve wracking. But he's right, too.

"It's their job to give a rat's ass about themselves. It's my job to give a rat's ass about myself," said Waylon, speaking with conviction. I am trying to look around the room, even from my limited vantage point, what with being under constant surveillance. I don't see anyone texting. We were actually *there*—present in the class. Weird. Being present is its own form of shock.

"Is that your rendition of the Golden Rule? Or the Disguised Shit Passing Itself Off for Gold(en) Rule?" asks Winter.

"Either way, I don't really care. But I'll take the five grand if I can get the five signatures. You can do whatever you want. Save the whales, or whatever." Waylon is like a thousand year-old sequoia, just a lot younger, not nearly as tall, and not a redwood.

"Thank you for weighing in, Mr. Waites. That's what we're doing here: expressing our views, and we're not always going to agree. In fact, it's more likely that we're never going to agree, but since we've got to live on the same planet, we've got to keep talking—and listening—or we'll never be able to respect each other enough to agree on a humane code of conduct. Does this make sense to everyone? This is not just an academic exercise. We're out to change ourselves, and in so doing, change the world. But you've got to start with yourself." I agree to start with myself so long as it does not involve any karaoke singing or other humiliating public displays. Come to think of it, I'll retract the last stipulation, or else I'd have to quit the cross-country team, which would probably be a good thing, but I'm not going to do it. I'm also probably not going to get a haircut, or join the NRA any time soon. I spaced it again. There's Winter, front and center.

"And I'm going to recommend putting listening first, *before* speaking. If you can't listen, you've got nothing to say. Before we wrap it up for today, I've got one final thought. We live in a capitalist society, right?" There are a few murmurs and generalized mumbling. "Let's break this down for a minute. What does it mean to live in a capitalist society? We like to say that it is the same as a free society, but is this really the case? Does capitalism always equal freedom? Could it be otherwise? What is the connection between capitalism and freedom?"

"It could be otherwise, but what do you mean? I don't get it." Rebecca Stoltzfus isn't the only one who doesn't get it. She doesn't get lots of stuff, but then again, that's true of most of the people in this room, maybe just about everyone, me included. LeBlanc probably gets it.

"Here's my proposition: you need capital in order to be a capitalist; capital is what makes you a capitalist; without capital you cannot be a capitalist but only a wanna-be capitalist, and God only knows there are wanna-be capitalists with no capital on every street corner—and probably jaywalking too. But wishing something doesn't make it so: you can't be a capitalist if you've got no capital. The people *without* the capital, in the most basic analysis, must spend their lives doing what the people *with* the capital tell them to do. How much capital do you need to be self-determining? Because what we're saying here is that in order to be free, that is, *really self-determining* and not just theoretically free, you need a shitload of capital, not just a six-month emergency fund. Most Americans—I'll repeat—*most* Americans have a net worth approaching zero—that is, after they take off everything they owe to the people *with* the money—*most* Americans have next to nothing. Over ninety-five percent of all American families have closer to zero than they do to six months of living expenses. How long could your family make it if, starting today, your family had *no* earned income?"

I am starting to feel depressed as hell. I am worth about $133.48, maybe less. In five years or so, after college, I'll just be in debt, trying to dig myself out with that two-pint shovel. And my parents aren't any better off than I am, in spite of working 25 years—each.

"Excuse me, Dr. Winter, like, what is capital?" It's Haley Cooper, the queen of the mean girls. I hope she didn't break a fake nail asking that really hard question. She's sitting in the front with her entourage. They're preparing for their world tour with Lady GagGag—in their minds. That's why some around here call her HaHa Shady. I'd go on tour with Lady GagGag, but I don't think I've got the bribe capital. Besides, Haley Cooper and her retinue will be all over the stage. Come to think of it, what the hell are they *doing* in this class? Maybe I'm wrong about them, but that would just be par for the philosophy course. Yeah, and what am I doing in here? Sometimes, I have no idea.

"Capital is, technically, money or property; but it is usually thought of merely as money. Capital is wealth. Without accumulated money or property, you can't actually be a capitalist." My heart is starting to feel lighter and lighter, since it's a good bet that I won't have to do any singing today. Harlan and Ferris are both yawning. Haley Cooper looks satisfied.

"My thesis," continues Winter, "based on this definition of capitalist, is simple: ninety-five percent of the American population are not capitalists *because they do not meet the minimum preconditions*, which would be the ability to live off of their accumulated wealth, in money and property, for over five years. The time stipulation is mine, and it should be longer, since after five years, you'll be groveling and sucking up to some capitalist, trying to scrape some capital out of selling your labor to a capitalist—if the job you're groveling for hasn't been sent to Manila or Bangalore, or simply eliminated by technology. *Self-determination requires sufficient capital to remain free*, something that a person without capital cannot do in a post-industrial technocratic society." After a final foray to the back of the class, Winter stops walking. He is right in front of the class. He scans the room like he's surveying the Promised Land. "Is this making any sense to anyone?" he asks, with furrowed brow. "Yes, Ms. LeBlanc, go ahead."

There's a pause and Monica clears her throat. "I think I get what you're saying, but five years seems kind of arbitrary, since you even admit that after five years, you'd be sucking up to the capitalist all over again. Why not make it longer? Even as long as you expect to live? Who would be left then?" Nice. Why didn't I think of that? Yeah, I think the questions are great—*after somebody else* comes up with them. Monica is almost too smart for this class. Weird.

Winter looked radiant. "Beautiful! Great question. Did everybody hear the question? If you had to live for the *rest of your life* on your existing accumulated assets, how many people would be able to make it? One out of a hundred? That might be it. Maybe even fewer. So it sounds like we're back to the 1%. Not too surprising, is it?" I hear a few books being put into knapsacks. Here we are again: pearls before swine. Welcome to planet earth. I'm afraid to put my books away, so I keep obliquely staring at Winter.

"Oh, I see, you clock-watchers. Okay, let's practice a phrase before we leave for today. Everybody listen and repeat: Do you want fries with that? Okay, let's hear it, loud and clear, or everybody's getting after-school suspension. One—two—three: *do you want fries with that?"* It was loud, no doubt, but apparently Winter wants us to go for more. "Again, louder, louder, let's go ladies and gentlemen! One—two—three: *do you want fries with that?*" Damn, that *was* loud. "Good, that's better. How many of you get to say that right now at your present job? Let's have a show of hands. Come on, get e'm up...seven people! Excellent. You other twenty—see what you've got to look forward to? That's what hell must be like—you repeat, 3000 times a day: *do you want fries with that?* And then you ask the same question day after day, for an eternity. And in this case, fifty years would constitute an eternity. So, I'll go back to a variation on my original question: if freedom exists in a capitalist society, who is actually free? Anybody?"

"The lucky dude with the capital, in money or property. We're the goddamn slaves." Holy shit, it is the mustard-sweatered Monica "Vera"

Leblanc once again, not putting her books away, a voice crying in the wilderness and not refusing to come forth. I am thinking about that mustard sweater, some powdered Gatorade, the cramp in my right ass cheek when…

"Bbbbbuuurrrrzzzzztt." It's the damn cattle call buzzer for the end of third period. Head down, I slavishly follow as the herd shuffles out of the room and into the feed lot leading to our fourth period classes. I cast a furtive glance out one of the few small windows as I pass them: the weather's shaping up for a good ten miler.

16

I AM EVERYTHING AND I AM NO THING
I AM ALL THINGS THAT MOVE AND DO
NOT MOVE

Tommie's footsteps echo between the ridges. His breathing is slow, easy, relaxed, purposive, polyrhythmic with the tapping of his feet. There is but a faint whisper of dawn. The morning is damp and calm, with infinite possibility. It is the time for waiting and the time for planning, the time for listening and the time for seeing, the time to tune in to the endless subterranean bass, the rhythmic pulsing of the essence of all things. Tommie makes his way through the labyrinthine course, first around the borough, and then within the forest. With each step, his mind seems to bear down upon its own focus, a focus that is yet to be realized by his consciousness. His mind is in the lead now, but not his consciousness. He follows the direction through the labyrinth, something he has done many times before, and now without trepidation.

A few dogs can be heard within the soundscape, a couple of them barking, and one howling for what he may never find. The sun has yet to tell of the nature of the day to come. The trees rise to their heights in anticipation. Tommie continues his purposive meandering. He could not sleep this night. His mind travelled through galaxies beyond his understanding; he could only observe and hope to know later, if the future ever comes. On nights such as this, he does what he must do: he soundlessly slips into his running gear and heads out the back door.

This time, it is a few hours before dawn. He has plenty of time for a slow, easy float through the town and forest that he's known all his life, to get a jump on seeing what may transpire this day, the day of the future that is the day of now. It's chilly but not cold, and as he warms to the thick still air he breaks a pleasant sweat, a sweat of the labor of all things. For a while, he is at one with his consciousness, but then he transcends his consciousness, to observe himself from the perch of an eagle, a raptor who maintains dignity from his lofty height and surveys his landscape before swooping down upon his prey. He becomes the red oak upon which the mighty bird of prey has landed, and from the oak he goes back to a time when only the red man stood upon this ground. The tree sees through the eyes of its ancestors a time before the foot print of the red man, a time before any foot prints at all, and it seems like an *augenblick*.

He becomes the insect on the tree, the mighty red oak that held the bird of prey upon its lofty perch, a small grasshopper listening for the time to decide. The grasshopper jumps into the tall prairie grass and makes its way to the nearby creek, the center of his universe. The earth smells sweet with an aroma of ten thousand lives, ten thousand ancestors, ten thousand moons. The grasshopper smells the sweetness of the ten thousand ten thousand and feels thankful. He becomes the small stream, barely audible but moving from the spring that touches the hidden aquifer, the source of life for the ten thousand, that for which the ten thousand would give all their silver and gold. The grasshopper drinks and is happy.

Tommie jumps the small stream on the small path in the pre-dawn wood where the eagle sits perched in the red oak, and Tommie is the stream. He is the grasshopper. He is the eagle. He is the red oak. He is all the ancestors of the stream, the grasshopper, the eagle, the red oak. He is at one with them all. He is even the rock that lines the banks of the small stream in the wood in the darkness of the hopeful morning. He is at one with the dawn of time. He is the dawn of time. He forgives all humans for their necessary sin of limited perspective, as he is forgiven.

Again he jumps the small stream in the wood, this time closer to the spring, near a grove of juniper trees, their blue-red berries waiting to nourish the inhabitants of the forest. May apples brush his feet to welcome him. The smell of birch trees mingles with the hemlocks. His consciousness has transcended time. He is no longer himself. He sees beyond the eagle, from a distant star, from another time and place, the troubles of all creatures here, and he feels an unbearable burden, the sorrow of all things. The interminable suffering of all things crushes his heart, an indelible pain. He feels the reverberations of the millions of hearts as they thump out their rhythm of life on the small planet that is home to them all. He goes beyond the beyond, transcending the sorrow itself, past the pain, past the broken hopes and dreams, past the suffering and crying out of man, turtle, eagle, deer, grasshopper, rabbit, coyote, bobcat, quail, stream, rock, and the earth itself, blood red. He flies above the treetops as his feet sink into the moist, red earth of his ancestors. He moves soundlessly. His ancestors grant him peace and safe passage. They watch from the eagle, as from the grasshopper. They watch as from the earth, blood-red. Above, the red tail hawk speaks to him. He hugs the earth as he flies through the forest, into the dawn of another day. He does not feel alone. As he looks at the earth flying by, dimly lit by a waning moon, tears well up his eyes. He feels the gratitude of all things, a timeless gratitude that is the ground bass for the endless orchestration and symphony of the spheres. Everything feels so close, and at the same time, so far, far away. He sees himself exit the wood, toward the sun behind the ridge and into the eternally new day.

17

SUBARU LEGACY

"Thanks for giving me a call." Tommie and Monica were at the Café de Ville, at a table in the back southwest corner, right beside the new mini-arboretum of multifarious potted plants, shrubs and trees. It was Saturday afternoon. Tommie had actually made the call. Not a whole lot like him, but last Saturday with Monica was anything but usual. He had on faded jeans, a dark green sweatshirt, and a retired pair of salty Asics, as per usual. His greasy black hair looked a little roostery, but compared to Monica's, it looked like he had just had it coiffed at a Parisian salon.

That morning, he had run a six-miler organized by Buffalo Bill, along with the rest of the guys on the cross-country team. They had run along the Conestoga River, and on the twisty, hilly, single track trails over the river bluffs. They had seen at least seven deer, including two fawns and a buck. The river was high. Skip and Jason planned on going out in kayaks with Kaitlin Ramsey and Brianna Colby after the six-miler. The last time they went out, they actually lost a kayak. Kriddle was along on that one, but it isn't exactly clear who lost the kayak. There's a rumor that it turned up a few days later in the Chesapeake Bay, and the team has been milking it ever since. Somebody put a picture of the alleged "found" kayak on Facebook and just about everybody's seen it, so now it's legendary.

Yeah, Ramsey and Mike Kriddle already broke up, right after that meet with Schuylkill Haven. It was an accident waiting to happen. Somebody should have gotten an Emmy for all that drama, but that's the burn of teenage love. They went out for something like twenty-seven days before the monster break up. For Kriddle, that's probably more days than all the other girls he's gone out with put together, plus about twenty-six days. And just like everybody else who has a cosmic breakup, he probably didn't learn his lesson.

The reality of it is that for most of the guys on the team, twenty-seven days is probably more days than all the girls they've gone out with— combined. Actually, if you leave out Skip "Running God" Garnet and Kenny "Sweet Boy" Zeferino, twenty-seven days is probably more days than *all* the rest of the guys have gone out on *all* their dates combined. Yeah, they're losers, but there are worse things. You still get to hang onto your youth if you don't have a pregnant girlfriend. And they're definitely trying to hang on to what's left of their youth.

Speaking of pregnant girlfriends, there's no way Kriddle got Kaitlin Ramsey pregnant, contrary to some of the specious talk around Pine Manor. Some of the guys on the team came to this conclusion after a lengthy conversation during the six-miler.   Needless to say, Kriddle wasn't involved. The impregnable logic supporting this conclusion, they argued, is fourfold: (1) Kriddle doesn't have the moves, (2) There's no way Ramsey would sleep with that ugly bastard, (3) Ramsey is Christian, so she's saving herself for marriage, and (4) Even if 1 – 3 weren't true, Kriddle's sperm count's gotta be like minus 5000, so there's no way he could get Nadine Rickmann pregnant—you know—the octomom, that chick that has about fourteen kids and no husband: there's success for you, if you want to be a dictator of a really small country. Anyway, the impending kayaking expedition also made for some excellent banter during the six-miler. Tommie himself even got an invitation for the float trip, but he turned it down. He had other plans.

Tommie gave Monica a call after practice. He was a little bit worried about Monica, but he wasn't going to bring it up in the hall at school. And he sure as hell wasn't going to bring it up during a free-for-all cross-country practice. He was glad he called.

"I didn't expect you to call, you know, after what happened last Saturday," Monica said softly.   Her voice exuded sincerity, unusual enough in itself.   She looked like she'd been awake for three days.

"Sure. I was a little bit worried about you. I mean, I know you're tough but still I was a little bit worried." It was true, but Tommie had no idea what to do about it. He had made the call anyway. Monica was beginning to realize that he actually did care, but she knew that he didn't have to care, that it wasn't his problem and he could bail out of the caring thing whenever he wanted to bail. However, her realization that he cared didn't answer her question concerning *why* he cared.

"You don't have to worry about me. But I do appreciate your concern."   Monica looked really tired, but her green eyes were clear—clear enough to be positively unnerving for Tommie. She didn't have on the mustard sweater. She was wearing black jeans, a pink cotton shirt, a jean jacket, and ankle-high Joe-Tec lightweight hikers. The fat plastic glasses were obscured by her voluminous and fantastically disheveled dirty brownish blonde hair.

"How is everything at home, with your mother, I mean?" Tommie wasn't sure if it was a good idea to bring up the elephant in the room, but he didn't know where else to start.

"Not… too good, Tommie, not too good…The doctors keep saying they got it all—I mean the cancer, but they said that before, and it turned out it wasn't true. It…wasn't…true. First, they said they only had to remove one side, but then, a few months and a dozen tests later, they had to remove the other side. Radiation, chemotherapy, it's such a blur. The reality is: nothing worked. That's all there is to it. Surgery's the only thing that's worked—*if* it's worked. It's really hard to remember the order of things or who said what, or if I'm imagining things, or reinterpreting, or inventing, or...I don't know. It's been a long twenty-three months. My mom's been so sick, it's almost like she isn't there." Monica suddenly had a surge of inspiration. "Hey... uhh...do you want to get out of here? I've got my license now, so I drove down."

"Ah, really? You drove down? Sure, I'd like to get out of here—if you want to. Sure. I don't think I can bear going through the process of ordering two drinks anyway, and I know it's my turn," said Tommie flatly, with a faint smile. He did, however, have fond memories of Monica's stupendous ordering skills.

"Yeah, let's just get the hell out of here." Monica stood up and fumbled through her purse for her car keys.

"Yeah, let's rip this joint." Tommie stood up just in time to avoid an ass cramp in his left cheek. He should have stretched a whole lot more after that trail run, but his attention was elsewhere. "Vera, did you borrow your parent's car?"

"No, actually, since I've got the part-time job at the University dining hall, I've got my own wheels. Nothing fancy, but my Dad helped me find it online. He didn't want me walking home by myself after dark. It's only a mile, but I see his point." Monica pointed to a rust-red nondescript sedan parked in the back of the small lot, right off High School Avenue. The thing was faded almost into oblivion.

"That's pretty cool." As they approached, Tommie could see that the driver's side front panel was crushed pretty good, but apparently it didn't affect the movement of the tire. As he walked around to the passenger side, he could see that the vehicle was also damaged on the passenger side front panel, and the passenger rear door had a massive dent as well.

"Yeah, it looks like shit, but they said it was safe. I guess nobody'll steal it, unless they're methheads. Then, you don't know *what* the hell they'll do. If they need it that bad, I guess I'll go back to walking."

"Good point. As long as it's mechanically sound and it gets you from point A to point B. Hey, this thing's a Subaru Legacy! My Dad had one of these back when we were kids. I remember it really well. Five-speed manual. Wow, Vera! *You've* got a five-speed manual! You can drive a stick shift? And you're a girl?" Tommie was remembering the time when the whole family went to the Columbia Drive-In Theater in their Subaru before they closed the place down a few years ago. Tommie couldn't have been more than seven or eight. Sammie spilled popcorn in the passenger's front seat at about the same time that Tommie spilled his drink in the driver's front seat while their parents, in the back seat, somehow didn't notice because there was some big scene going on up there on the screen and they weren't noticing much of anything going on right then in the car. And since Tommie and Sammie couldn't even understand how their parents could *see* the screen from the back seat, they took the lack of perception as a sign that they should act as if nothing happened, which they did. That meant that neither could move nor make any attempt to clean up the mess. That worked great until their dad had to get into the driver's seat to drive home, sitting in nearly a quart of sticky ass beverage, while their mom simultaneously sat in the carnage of a large popcorn. Then, when their dad started yelling and their mom hit her head trying to jump back out of the car like she'd sat on a snake, both Tommie and Sammie couldn't hold back the laughter. What was so good about the memory was that all four of them ended up laughing, especially when they saw both Dad's and Tommie's soda-soaked butts back at the house.

Tommie knew there was fake-buttery popcorn in that car for years after the event—with the stench to prove it—a stench that smelled something like a dozen rancid oiled down baseball gloves. Tommie also remembered the event with some sense of longing and wistfulness, since he couldn't remember doing much as a family after that, and it was so, so long ago. Where did all the time go, and what were they all so busy doing to fill it? He couldn't even remember what movie was playing. Then Tommie noticed that Monica was staring at him, wondering where he'd gone.

"Watch it, Tommie Boy. I might drive you to an undisclosed location and…"

"And what?"

"I can cook too."

"You can cook, you can drive a stick shift, and you're a girl? What planet are you from?"

Monica was smiling, a smile like Tommie had never seen before. "Well, I *know* that *you're* from Uranus. That's already been established. For the time being, my planet shall remain a mystery."

"Sure, as long as you can cook. What year is this thing?"

"I have no idea. Who cares?" Monica looked duly nonplussed. "Old. Old enough to afford. Would you like to hear about my burlap sack collection?"

"Okay, I get the message. I'm boring you. Humor me. Just hold on a minute. Let me check." Monica was getting ready to turn the key in the ignition, but she paused. Tommie got out, walked around to the driver's side, and opened the door. Monica slowly leaned forward and put her forehead on the dash.

"Stay where you are, Vera. Don't pass out. I'm just checking the door panel. It's a 1993 Subaru Legacy L sedan, manufacture date 09/1992. This model is one of the last two-wheel drive models that Subaru made before they switched over to All Wheel Drive. This one's front wheel drive, plenty good enough, unless you've got a trailer full of dead bodies and you're driving on an icy road toward South Mountain."

Monica leaned back in her bucket seat, staring at Tommie. "Awesome. You're starting to scare me. You know way too much about my car. What are you gonna do next, tell me its astrological sign? Now get back in and let's get the hell out of here. Unless you want to spend some time *alone* with the car."

"That won't be necessary. All I need to do is check the odometer." Tommie gets back in, leans over, and then buckles up. "247,496 miles. Wow. I like the mechanical odometer so much better than those damn digital things. For one, they go out on you, and secondly, you can't see the mileage without turning on the ignition. This thing'll last you until you graduate from college and get a decent job, and then you won't have to worry." Monica was leaning back in her seat, face to the roof, the look of resignation on her face.

"Yeah, I won't have to worry, my ass. I know you're from Uranus, but are you serious? Here's more like what'll happen. I'll graduate after four years from a second rate school with $47,000 in student loan debt, after I, as they say, worked my way through college, and then I'll work thirty-seven hours a week at Dull-Mart with no benefits while I'm looking for a real job. I'll be looking for a real job for two years. The entire time, people will keep telling me that I should be thankful to have a job at all. I'll keep looking for a real job, but the real job I might have had was outsourced overseas in 2008, but I'll never know that, so I'll keep looking. I'll be pulling down $13,210 take home a year while I'm paying back $420 a month for ten years at 5.25 percent on the student loans, and I'll be collecting $214 a month in food stamps. Luckily, I will have found a 175-square-foot studio apartment that I can afford, even if the roof leaks a little and the neighborhood ain't anything to write home about. After the student loan payment, I'll be raking in $8170 a year, just a little bit less than I could make as a beggar. I'll take a second job working nights twenty hours a week at Broken Family Dollar. You know you're a serf when you're working for Broken Family Dollar." Tommie's mouth is half open like he's getting ready to speak, but nothing comes out. He looks dazed. He tries again.

"...Wow...I mean, wow."

"Don't stop me now, bro. I'm just getting started. Not to worry, if I'm a *really good* girl and don't take any vacations or spend money on anything I don't absolutely need, the entire student loan debt will be paid off by the time I'm thirty-two, so I'll get to keep all of my after-tax salary at Dull-Mart and Broken Family Dollar! And, I'll have gotten a raise at Dull-Mart by then, bumping up my take home to $1300 a month! And as long as my 1993 Subaru keeps running and they don't jack up my insurance rates more than two hundred percent, I won't even have to walk to work! Finally, my B.A. in English, French and Culture Studies will certainly not have gone to waste, since when I order my weekly beverage at the Café de Ville, I'll be able to read the menu and actually pronounce all that shit. Where's the downside?"

Tommie looks doubtful.

"It'll never happen, Vera. Never happen."

"Why not, Tommie? Don't you believe in the American Dream?"

"I'm telling you Vera. It'll never happen."

"Why not, Tommie, Oh Oracle of Truth, seer of the future?"

"Because they will have cut the food stamp program by then."

Monica started to laugh a cynical laugh, a laugh rife with despair. "You've got me there. I guess I'll have to take a third job over at Twinky City. That totally sucks."

"That's a good one, but Twinky City will probably be shut down by then. Yeah, no doubt. It'll be shut down. Sorry. Alright...let's get out of here. I'm ready to go. Does this car actually run, or did you just have it towed over here to make an impression?"

"You *know* I'm all about making an impression. That's me, a poser." Tommie noticed there was a hole about the size of a chipmunk in the dash, right above the glove box. He thought it was immensely funny.

"This here is one hell of a car, pardner, ain't it?" he quipped. Monica turned her head, slowly, toward him.

"Shore 'nuff is. Git yoself ready, boy. We's gonna be takin' a whild rhide."

Monica turns the key and the thing shakes as it hums to life. She fishes around for reverse and then lets the clutch out ever so slowly. The car still manages to lurch and shudder its way through the thirty or so feet before she pushes in the clutch, hits the brake, puts it in first, and starts the slow process of again releasing the clutch. The sound of gears winding, meshing, grinding like ghosts with their ever-so-faint howls. Uneven, jerky forward motion propels them to the street. It's a good thing that they didn't actually eat anything before they got into this bucking bronco. Tommie kept looking around at the inside of the car, it's weird-ass automatic shoulder seat belts that'll give you a licking if you're not sitting right there in place when you turn the key, and the sagging, stained roof liner that was, to Tommie, really stylin'.

"Hey, how does somebody get stains like that on the roof liner? They don't look like water stains to me." Then he thought he'd better shut up, what with Monica looking like she had her hands full just keeping the baby in gear and on the road.

"Dude, I just got this thing. I've only had it like three weeks. How the hell would I know? Besides, do you really want to think about it? I don't. Anyway, I kind of like the pattern. It's like tie-dye or something." Monica was gripping the wheel with both hands, so hard that it was like she was on a trapeze clinging for dear life.

"Oh yeah, real Woodstocky. It takes me right back to when things were cool. Not like I remember when that was. Definitely not like now.

I mean, who can get that feeling in a 2010 American Motors product? Not gonna happen."

"Now you're feelin' the vibe," said Monica, who seemed pleased, at least at the moment. She was leaning forward and squinting out the windshield. Concentrating on not wrecking was taking her mind off everything else.

"The 247K doesn't hurt when you're talking about the vibe. In fact, it's got such a vibe that everything looks blurry in the sideview mirror. That's a classic touch," said Tommie. Monica was bumping and jerking along George Street. She was up to second gear, and the speedometer registered an optimistic twenty-one miles per hour. Tommie knew he should shut up, but he couldn't help himself.

"Ah, a cassette deck comes included with your classic vehicle. Nice. Very nice. Does it work, or is it just for show?"

Monica frowned but kept her eyes on the road.

"It works, Tommie," she said, exasperated. "Look on the floor behind the seats. I've got some cassettes from my dad back there. And I found a couple in the car when we bought it. At least the thing doesn't have an eight track. If you think this thing is funny, you should have seen my dad's '76 Renault 12 with the eight track he put in it back in the day. We all called it the '12' because we didn't know if it was pronounced Re-nault or Re-know. Can you believe that? So we just called it the '12'. Kind of stupid, right? Actually, I still don't know if it's Re-nault or Re-know. That thing had an eight track. I think my dad put it in himself after he got it, under the dash. I'm not sure, since I wasn't around then, but it sure looked like it. You'd be groovin' and right in the middle of a song: silence. Then bbbzzzuuuurrrrrrppppt: silence. Then it would start right back up on the next track in the middle of the same song. Real fancy. Whoever heard of a Motown song with an intermission? Ain't no way you can stop that shit without ruining the groove. Marvin Gaye, Sly and the Family Stone, the Jackson Family, Rare Earth, Stevie Wonder, Rick James, Earth Wind and Fire, War? Oh, and Aretha Franklin. Soul music with an intermission? No way."

"Yeah, you're right. That would totally screw the groove. Totally. I couldn't take it. It could give you a complex if you kept hearing the groove and then—bam—silence—the groove gets cut right off and you're hanging right there on that sonic cliff and suddenly—bam—out of nowhere, the groove slams back. That's just plain traumatic, if you ask me. That's probably why I've got Post-Traumatic-Sonic-Disorder. It's bad, Vera, it's bad. In the groove—slam—silence— bzzzuurrrppt—bam—in the groove. God, I've got

PTSD! Help! Help me! That's monster traumatic, if you ask me, I know."

Monica was leaning forward, squinting, about as close to the windshield as she could get without catapulting right through it. "I'm not asking, Tommie Boy. I've got the picture. I know you're still screwed up from when it happened to you. It's obvious. You're groovin' big time and the bam—silence—bzzzuurrrppt—silence—bam—you're back in the groove. That *could* screw *you* up for life. I know it did screw *you* up for life. You're just a sensitive guy."

Monica, meanwhile, was jerking the hell out of the transmission. It felt to Tommie like she was engaging and disengaging the clutch like one hundred times every mile, but when Tommie looked down at her left leg, it was just shaking and barely touching the top of the pedal, just in case she needed to jam it on down. Maybe it was the car. It felt to him like a mule with attitude. Not like Tommie had ever been *on* a mule, but that's what he imagined it felt like. It seemed like the attitude part was a given. He looked back between the seats and started fumbling on the floor. He found six cassette tapes. Two of them were actually in plastic covers.

"Hey, here's Elton John from...1975. Holy crap. It's an antique." The cassette was clear and had no cover.

"Well pop it in, runner dude. All I need are more distractions. I don't know where the hell we're going anyway." The car had entered a vibrating rhythm all its own, at twenty-four miles per hour. Monica's hands were whitish, knuckles up, at ten and two.

Tommie seemed oblivious. "Does anybody? Okay, I'll put it in."

"Now don't go getting all philosophical on me now, Dr. Winter. Fifty-one minutes five times a week is about all I can take."

"C'mon, you *know* you like it." He was trying to get the cassette tape in the player but he had it upside downside. It wasn't going anywhere.

"Tommie, that's backwards, dude. Flip it around." Monica was taking her eyes off of the road for a dangerously long time. Tommie, now aware of the precariousness of the situation, was starting to grit his teeth. Monica needs practice— a lot more practice, he thought. Monica started to swerve, then overcorrected and he thought his life had flashed before him, but if it did, it was a blank. She corrected the overcorrection. He felt his adrenaline really kick in. He forgot about the precious Elton John cassette as it fell out of his hands and onto the floor by his feet. The next thing he knew, they were driving right off the right side of the road and onto the grassy knoll leading up to the high school. Tommie looked over at

Monica, who was pushing both of her feet flat to the floor, gripping the wheel tightly with both hands, eyes really, really big. Suddenly, she didn't look tired at all. She was pushing in the clutch, but she missed the brake and was inadvertently putting the pedal to the metal. 6500 freakin' RPMs, noted Tommie—*with* the clutch in. Luckily, they were riding up a gentle embankment, and within seventy-five feet they coasted to a stop. Monica quickly dumped it into neutral, hit the brake and stared straight ahead like she was looking for the total eclipse of the sun. A good ten seconds of silence. Then Tommie looked over at Monica, her fat plastic glasses and dirty brownish-blonde Picasso totally obscuring her visage.

"Are you okay?" asked Tommie. Monica stared straight ahead. He asked again. "Monica, are you okay?" Monica spoke at half-volume.

"You're not gonna say anything to my parents, are you? You're not, right?"

"I'll just tell 'em I distracted you, and you couldn't help but coast into the grassy knoll. Anyway, it wasn't a wreck. It was just a leisurely coast up the grassy knoll."

"Yeah, thanks a lot. That'll make it *so* much better." She hadn't lost her edge.

"You're welcome. Hey, I just thought of something else that's really awesome about your car."

"It smells like diapers full of shit?"

"No, but that's a plus too. I was thinking that in the unlikely event that you *do* run into something, you won't even be able to tell, what with the pre-existing customized fancy body work."

"I'll give you some fancy body work. Now we've got to back this thing off the grass without getting stuck and before the cops drive by." Monica was now out of her stupor, doing some 360 degree recon. All clear.

"We? Good luck with that. Thanks for the ride. I think I can walk home from here." Tommie looked at the hole in the dash and almost burst out laughing.

"Very funny. Now look back there and make sure I don't back out when something's coming." Both of them were over the adrenaline rush and it already seemed pretty funny. It'll probably seem even funnier in twenty years, if they live that long. In thirty years, it'll be hilarious. Monica managed to back it out with only a minor grind or two, and they headed east. Tommie was still fumbling with the cassette.

"Now where, car nut?" Monica said, apparently fully recovered.

"We could take a walk down by the river. The trails aren't muddy today, and the temperature's perfect." He got the cassette in.

"Great idea, Tommie. I can't say I've spent a lot of time wandering on those trails, but if you know where you're going, cool." In spite of her voice, Monica was still imperceptibly trembling from her first off-road escapade. Her chin was almost on top of the steering wheel.

"Don't worry. You'll like it. I won't get us lost."

"Hey, great, but first we've got to *actually* make it there..."

Duh—duh duh duh duh duh duh duh duh— —duh duh duh duh duh duh duh duh....

"Someone Saved My Life Tonight! Yes!" Monica looked almost happy.

Suddenly the cassette player began to emit a weird noise. The weird noise grew louder.

"Shit! It ate the tape. It ate the tape," Monica blurted out.

"Hey, maybe not...okay, yeah, it...ah....ate the tape..." Tommie was attempting to pull what was left of the cassette tape out of the archaic tape player. He carefully pulled the unraveled tape out of the player. "So much for Elton John."

"I'll say. But that was a hell of a song. Oh well, the car's still moving. How about the radio? If we can stand it. Try the radio. Play something that doesn't suck."

"That could be tough, but I'll see what I can do." Tommie fumbled with the dial for three blocks. No digital. Nothing that doesn't suck. Nothing that doesn't suck. Is it possible? he asked himself. And then... amidst the static, they heard the unmistakable voice...

The sun is sinking low/And I don't know where I'm going to go...

"Hey, *Humanoid* by Madame Xero! Tune it in and leave it on, Tommie. Leave it on."

"Yeah, sure. Oh, yeah, the power ballad of all time. This *definitely* doesn't suck."

They headed south to the river.

"Turn it up, Tommie. Turn it up." He turned it up and the speakers rattled. He backed it off to the edge of the rattle. Perfect.

You're telling me you're here to stay/But where where where am I?

The wail of the trombone and bass clarinet slithered through the vintage sound system, and then the moan of the steel guitar.

Monica got it into third for a minute, lost her nerve, and downshifted. They kept bucking toward Creek Drive...

...I'm running just to stay in place/Of my humanity, not a trace...

...and parked near the S-bend under the forest canopy at the end of the dirt road.

The moon is up, the wood is still/But I stay

up to make my kill...

Monica turned off the engine and the sounds of the forest were everywhere.

It really was a beautiful day. They could hear more birds than they could count or even notice, and when they looked up, there was a whole other world up there. In a way, it was too bad that they had to stay down below on terra firma, but everything has its place, and today they were amidst the thousands of acres of temperate forest in the late summer, along the S-bend in the river as it slowly meandered south to empty, finally, into the Chesapeake Bay. Millions of unsung organisms, both great and small, lived in this watershed. Monica and Tommie were a part of the rhythm of life as they walked through the maze of endless forest trails, trails used more by the forest inhabitants than by the occasional human visitors.

Woodpeckers had left their marks in the dead trees along the trail, most of which were still looking skyward. They encountered a box turtle on the trail in front of them, head outstretched to assess the danger. The sound of the river was a part of the interminable ground bass, a sound that telegraphed the vibrancy of life, the feeling that their moment was but fleeting, while the bass ostinato echoed on beyond reckoning. Tommie and Monica were seamlessly enveloped within something far larger than themselves, far larger than any single perspective, something the truth of which would be perceivable only in theory, if ever, which is to say, not perceivable. Their conversation was swallowed up in the sounds of the forest. They were grafted into the forest, but they were not lost. They walked for a good ten minutes in silence. Neither looked at the other but were lost in amazement at all that was around them. Finally, Tommie spoke.

"I'm really sorry about your mother, Monica. It isn't fair."

"Thanks, Tommie. I agree, it isn't fair, to her or to Dad or me. She's been ripped off and I feel really ripped off, but what can we do? What can *I* do?" Her voice had an earnestness that was usually submerged beneath her cynicism.

"You've been doing everything you can, and I'm sure your mom and dad appreciate it, even if it doesn't seem like it."

"Yeah, I know, but it's not really making it better. My mom took off fall semester 2009, and she thought she would be back teaching last spring. But then they found cancer on the other side, so she had to take off last spring too. Now, they've found some other complications, and they say stuff like 'we thought we got it all, but now the tests indicate that it's somewhere else in her system, but we can't say where.' Really informative." Monica's voice sounded thin and distant, like she was trying hard to keep the pain at bay, but with little success. They walked side by side on what looked like an old logging road.

"Anyway, she hasn't taught a class at the University since June summer session 2009, almost fifteen months. She was on paid medical leave, but that was only for one year. Since the start of this semester, she's been on unpaid medical leave. They've already got adjuncts teaching her courses. The adjuncts get about one-third the pay that Mom was getting—that's what I heard—and it's not like *she* was raking it in. Where's the incentive for the University to keep her on, especially since image and money, rather than quality, seem like their key concerns? I'm afraid they're going to try to find a way to get rid of her, or at least cut her off of the medical insurance. It really hurts when it feels like they just want to throw her away. What kind of world is this, anyway? What kind of world...?" Her voice trailed off into its own non-answer. They continued to walk within sight of the river on the increasingly narrow, undulating trail.

"Can they do that?"

"Let's just say, from what I can see, they can do just about whatever they want to do, and they'll get away with it, if you don't have a lot of time, money, and resources to fight them—the three things that you don't have when you're already down. I'm sure you get what I'm driving at." Monica's voice was filled with despair, exasperation, and a palpable sense of gradual asphyxiation.

"Yeah, but there's gotta be something. There's *gotta* be…" Tommie paused, unable to find anything that sounded even remotely comforting to say, and then continued. A blanket platitude was about all he could muster. "Well, hopefully, everything will work out and you won't have to keep worrying about any of this." He felt some shame for his pathetic attempt to comfort Monica.

"Yeah, hopefully, but I've hoped for a lot of stuff since all this started, and most of it never came true. I even prayed about everything, and Mom is *still* sick and she *still* can't work and Dad hasn't gotten a decent night's sleep in months. Come to think of it, neither have I. How long can that go on? It just wears you down, little by little, until you think that you can't fight it anymore. And I'm not even the one who's sick." Monica's voice cracked. They had to walk single file now, as the trail had narrowed, with Tommie in front. The both looked down at the path ahead, slowly walking south on the trail the locals called the Susquehannock Trail.

"Is your mom getting any better, or is it

impossible to tell?"

Monica took a deep breath and let out a long sigh. "Well, it *seemed* like she was, but with the new tests, like I said, now they're saying that she's still got cancer somewhere in her system. They didn't get it all out with the double mastectomy. You know, the removal of her breasts." Tommie winced. He hoped Monica didn't notice. She gave no indication that she did, and continued to explain the situation to Tommie. "It's hard to say just what her symptoms actually are, when the treatments make her so sick. It's like when she gets the treatments, she has no life. She's too sick to have a life, and if they don't work, then her life was over when the treatments started, only we didn't know it. It's like she's been hollowed out from the pain. It really makes me wonder who's in charge of the universe. "

"Yeah, I hear you. Is there anything I can do?"

"You're doing it, Tommie, you're doing it."

"What exactly am I doing?"

"You're listening. You're there. That's everything you need to do."

Tommie doubted that he was doing much of anything that made any real impact. "Well, I can do that. I might not be the world's greatest listener, but I can do it."

"You're not the world's greatest karaoke singer either, but you can do it. You know I saw you do it in Winter's class. That was beautiful." Monica leaned forward and punched Tommie, lightly, on his left shoulder blade. He stopped and turned around, looking her in the eye. Even at such a horrible time for her, Monica managed to smile. Tommie smiled back but felt a great void of helplessness on the verge of hopelessness. He fought it off and turned back to the trail.

"It was about as beautiful as your driving. Only my singing wasn't a hazard to life and limb."

"That's your opinion. My ears and cerebellum will never be the same."

"I think the brain damage was a pre-exisiting condition." Monica punched Tommie in the right shoulder, a pretty decent slug too. Again, Tommie turned around, stopping.

"Owww! Hey, watch it! I didn't know you were going to resort to violence just to suppress the truth!"

"That's less than you deserve, but I'm letting you off easy since you had to ride over here with me."

"Oww. Oww. Oww. There goes my cross-country season. Thanks a lot."

"Right. Your season was over the minute you stepped out on that course."

"Oww. Oww. Oww. Now you're hurting

my feelings."

"Would you rather have me hit you again?"

"Those are my choices? Somehow, I feel like I'm back in Winter's class. Or at the very back of the pack in a cross-country race. I'll lay off if you lay off. Deal?"

"Okay, it's a deal. Truce." They kept walking along the western bank of the river. It wasn't long before they saw a great blue heron in a small inlet, out of the way of the main current. It must have been fishing for supper.

"Look Monica! Shhh." Tommie pointed through the trees along the bank. They crouched, froze in place, and stared. The staring went on for some time.

"Now that's a freakin' big bird. It's so big it's almost scary," Monica whispered.

"That's probably the same thing that bird is thinking about us right now, and hoping we get the hell out of here so that it can get itself a nice fish dinner."

"Those things like fish?" asked Monica, intrigued.

"Well they don't like crabs, oysters, lobster, crayfish, barnacles and scallops, as far as I know. They don't like shellfish at all. But they do like a nice tasty sunfish. I've also heard they track the chupacabra." Tommie looked serious.

Suddenly, he felt another punch, this time a blow to his left shoulder. The bird heard the interlopers and started looking around. Its perimeter had been compromised. Then it started the laborious process of flapping its wings to get off the river. Within seconds, it was gliding south.

"Owww. Owww. Owww. Good thing I don't hit girls. Especially girls that drive '93 Subarus."

"You're such a Mother Teresa. How can you live with yourself?" asked Monica, gradually standing.

"It's easy if I don't look in the mirror and see my halo." It was usually obvious that neither one spent much time in front of a mirror, a fact often pointed out by classmates at Pine Manor. Tommie got up and they headed back down the Susquehannock Trail.

"Yeah, you might be blinded by the light."

"*You* might be blinded by the light. I'm impervious, being a saint and all."

"Is Mother Teresa a saint already? You're the one in Nussbaum's AP History, not me." It was true: Tommie was in Nussbaum's Advanced Placement Post-Enlightenment History, whereas Monica was in Sturrock's regular section. They hadn't covered the possible sainthood of Mother Teresa in either class, not even in Nussbaum's AP History.

"Probably not, what with all the machinations at the Vatican. There are a lot of Pontifications going on, but it usually still takes about three hundred years to get anything done. Maybe she's got special status, and she'll move up in the year 2482, after 470 more years of councils. Don't want to rush things. It's a big deal if you're going to turn somebody into a saint. I mean, what if you're wrong? What if they were just faking it and they duped a lot of people, and the evidence is scant, falsified, anecdotal, and you used it to grant them sainthood? Is sainthood reversible, like my Totes raincoat? I think not."

"Well, if those Vatican dudes make a mistake, maybe they could just destroy the evidence and nobody'll be the wiser," said Monica.

Maybe she's onto something, thought Tommie. "Maybe? Hey, it's not just the church. They're pretty good techniques for anybody in power. Suppression. Destruction. Falsification. Denunciation. Burning at the stake. They sound like the standard procedures, and they probably worked great for about 1700 years, but now Julian Assange would probably have the incriminating evidence posted on Wikileaks before those canonizers had time to eat lunch. They'd have to skip lunch and try to intercept the evidence. Not an easy thing to do. Especially if you haven't had lunch."

Monica burst out laughing. "That was funny, Tommie. That was funny. It's not an easy thing for *me* to skip lunch, I can tell you that," she said. "If I do skip it, it's all I think about. If I don't skip it, I forget about it as soon as I didn't skip it. Then I start thinking about snack time before dinner, and then right after that I'm thinking about dinner. It sucks."

"When you've got low blood sugar, it's hard not to think about eating. Come to think of it, it's hard not to think about eating even when you *don't* have low blood sugar."

"Yeah, Tommie, you've got that right. I think I've got low blood sugar right now. Wanna go to the Sugar Bowl and get some fries and stuff?"

Tommie stopped walking and turned around. "With you? Or are you going to drop me off so I can get some peace and quiet?" Monica looked like she was going to hit Tommie yet again. "Sure, okay, okay, I'll go over there with you if you don't hit me too many times. Plus, you're going to have to actually *drive* over there. Do you think you can make it?"

"Hey, Tommie. We made it over here, didn't we? Besides, if you don't like my ride, you can always walk, and I'll see you over there in about an hour."

"Oh yeah, feel the love. I wouldn't miss your ride for anything. But now, we've got to get back to the car. Hopefully, it's still there."

"What's that supposed to mean?"

"Maybe Ferris and Harlan followed us and pushed it into the river. For our own safety."

"You've been watching too many forensic files."

"Or too few. And, we've still got to get the hell out of this forest," Tommie said.

"Well, don't just stand there. Start walking back, Sherpa guide. Unless you're waiting to get beamed back to your planet."

Tommie and Monica meandered back on the hilly trails along the river bluffs until they saw the crumpled rust colored freedom machine in the clearing at the end of the dirt lane.

"Wanna listen to the radio on the way back, Vera? Maybe we can catch them playing *Humanoid* again. It's on heavy rotation."

"Oh yeah!"

As they drove out of the wood, you could almost hear the whisper echo through the valley…

Sublimely staged, I lie in wait/To slay the child, don't hesitate…

I walk with blood upon my hands/Impersonating, yes, a man…

The time for peace has long since gone/As I waylay the restless throng…

The mass who try to fill their mouths/With victuals to keep their health...
Alas, it's now too late to see/To think, to act, to love, to be...
The moon is down, the wood is still/But I stay up to make my kill...

It wasn't long before the whine of the Subaru was lost in the wind.